THE PALOMINO MYSTERY

THE PALOMINO MYSTERY

BY ANN SHELDON

WANDERER BOOKS
Published by Simon & Schuster, New York

Copyright © 1962 by Stratemeyer Syndicate
All rights reserved
including the right of reproduction
in whole or in part in any form
First Wanderer edition, 1981
Published by WANDERER BOOKS
A Simon & Schuster Division of
Gulf & Western Corporation
Simon & Schuster Building
1230 Avenue of the Americas
New York, New York 10020

Designed by Becky Tachna
Manufactured in the United States of America
10 9 8 7 6 5 4 3

WANDERER and colophon are trademarks
of Simon & Schuster

LINDA CRAIG is a trademark of Stratemeyer Syndicate,
registered in the United States Patent and Trademark Office

Library of Congress Cataloging in Publication Data

Sheldon, Ann.
Linda Craig, the palomino mystery.

Published in 1962 under title: Linda Craig and the
palomino mystery.
SUMMARY: Linda's search for the perfect palomino
leads her to a dangerous encounter with modern-day horse
thieves.
[1. Horses—Fiction. 2. Mystery and detective stories]
I. Title. II. Title: The palomino mystery.
PZ7.S5413Lk 1981   [Fic]   80-39846

ISBN 0-671-42649-4
ISBN 0-671-42650-8 (pbk.)

Contents

Mysterious Lights 1

"Come on, Speedy!" Linda Craig coaxed the sleek bay horse. "Nod your head!"

The slim, sixteen-year-old brunette, dressed in blue shirt and tan levis, moved a cupped hand toward the nostrils of the horse. But the cue failed. Speedy jerked his head aside, wheeled in the corral, and trotted off a few steps.

With a sigh, Linda turned to her tall brother Bob, eighteen, seated on the top rail of the corral fence. His sandy hair and a sprinkling of freckles indicated the two Craigs' Scottish background, while Linda reflected their Spanish ancestry.

"Bob, I'm doing exactly what I read in the training manual," Linda insisted. "I guess Speedy'll never be a trick horse!"

Bob grinned. "Maybe Speedy should learn to read the book."

Linda laughed. Dark eyes flashing mischievously,

she tossed her wavy hair. "What would you suggest, Brother dear? Sending him to school?"

"You'll have to ask Cactus Mac," Bob answered. "He's the expert here on Rancho del Sol."

Bob tilted his cowboy hat forward to shade his brown eyes against the May sun, and scanned the ranch for a sign of Cactus, the foreman. Rancho del Sol, better known to Southern Californians as Old Sol, stretched for acres on all sides of the main house.

Linda's eyes, too, roved over the pasture where horses and cattle grazed on the lush grass. Presently her gaze turned toward the hacienda, the long, low ranch house lying in the shade of six giant oak trees. Patches of sunlight glinted off the white adobe walls and red tile roof. Beyond stood the water tank on high stilts with a windmill beside it. Nearby was the barn.

"I love it here," Linda said. "Oh, there's Cactus Mac now," she added, pointing to a bandy-legged man who strode briskly from the barn. "Cactus, please come here!" she called.

The foreman hurried over and listened to Linda's complaint about Speedy.

"Wal now," Cactus drawled, "let me tell you something about Speedy thar." The foreman ran his tongue across his lips. "He's one of the best cuttin' horses I've ever known. Just turn him loose in a herd, and he'll cut out a good beef whether thar's a rider directin' him or not. That's what he was

trained to do, and it makes sense to him. Forcin'
Speedy to nod his head up and down for no purpose
don't appeal to his savvy."

"I guess what you really mean," said Linda, "is
that I'm not a very good trainer."

"Didn't say that," Cactus Mac replied quickly.
"You shouldn't expect any horse, no more'n any
person, to do all things. If you want to teach a horse
tricks, you get yourself a pleasure horse, and it'll
plumb love doin' tricks."

As the foreman went off, Linda turned to Speedy,
took off the halter, and gave the animal a pat. She let
down the bars into the pasture. "Go cut out a beef
for yourself!"

Speedy eyed the opening, then bolted through it
to freedom. He kicked up his heels, arched his back
in a leap, and galloped off to join the other horses.
Linda draped herself over the corral fence and
looked into space.

"What are you thinking about?" Bob asked her.

"A golden palomino of my very own," she answered dreamily. "A young one that I can teach to
do tricks."

"Why a palomino?"

"Because that's a Spanish breed," Linda replied.
She clasped her hands earnestly. "It'll understand
me and I'll understand the pony. I guess that's the
Spanish in me."

Linda's and Bob's great-great-grandfather, Don
Fernando Perez, and his beautiful wife Rosalinda,

had come from Spain as bride and groom to this California ranch. The oldest daughter in each generation since then had been named Rosalinda. But Rosalinda Craig had been nicknamed Linda.

To her secret delight, she looked just like pictures of her famous great-great-grandmother, but unlike her furbelowed ancestor, Linda always wore simply styled or tailored clothes.

As she stood mulling over the idea of owning a palomino, the ranch's coyote-shepherd dog, Rango, began to bark. Linda and Bob looked up. Coming along the lane to the hacienda was a lone horseman.

"High stepper," Bob commented as the glistening golden-chestnut Morgan approached, head erect, its gait in perfect rhythm.

"Looks like a show horse," Linda replied.

In a few minutes the strange rider came toward the corral. He was about thirty-five years old, had clean-cut features and a pleasant smile.

Bob had already swung his long legs over the top rail of the fence and dropped to the ground. "May I help you?" he asked the stranger.

"I'm looking for my friend, Mr. Tom Mallory," the tall, gray-eyed caller stated with a smile. "Is he here?"

"Not at the moment," Bob replied, and introduced himself and Linda. "Bronco went into town this morning, but he expected to be back by now."

"Bronco?" the rider inquired with a grin.

Linda laughed. "Our grandfather has had that

nickname since childhood, when he tried to imitate the antics of the ranch's broncs."

"I see," the rider said. "I'm John Davis, on vacation up here from Los Angeles. I have a mystery for your grandfather to solve."

Mystery! Linda and Bob were alert at once to hear it. But they were forced to wait. The sound of a jeep announced the arrival of Bronco Mallory.

The jeep stopped with a squeal of rubber and Tom Mallory stepped out. He was a big man, whose sombrero made him look even taller than his six feet. He had iron-gray hair, a ruddy tan face, and friendly blue eyes.

Bronco grinned and pumped his friend's hand. "Johnny, you jet birdman, where'd you come from?"

"Ditched my plane for a couple of weeks to roam around on this horse. Prince Brownlee, meet *Bronco* Mallory and his granddaughter and grandson."

The horse shook his head and snorted. Linda thought, *He* knows how to respond to commands.

John Davis said he was browsing around the countryside to get the feel of ranch life again. "I'm staying at the Brownlees and borrowed this prize-winner from them."

Linda walked around the horse, noting its regular breathing, good conformation, and sound legs. She liked the way he pawed the ground with his right front hoof, shaking his head at the same time.

11

He must be used to taking bows, Linda thought.

Bronco asked Linda and Bob to water Prince Brownlee and tether him in a shady spot by the barn. While they were gone, Tom Mallory led the way to the house.

"Linda and Bob have come to live with my wife and me," he said. "Their parents were killed in an accident a few months ago."

"Not your daughter Rosalinda?" Johnny asked, shocked.

"Yes." Tears glistened in Bronco's eyes. "It unnerved all of us. Her husband was a major in the army. The children fortunately had always spent their summers here, so this is a second home to them. They're excellent riders and Linda is sure daft about horses. Bob attends engineering college. He's real handy at repairing tools and machinery."

Johnny expressed his sympathy, then asked, "How are you and your wife?"

"We're both well, thanks. Let's go up to the house, Johnny."

Linda and Bob were coming from the barn as John Davis called to them. "I want you to hear about the mystery. Perhaps you can help solve it."

The four seated themselves in sturdy redwood chairs on the shaded patio, and Linda leaned forward eagerly to hear the story.

"As you know, Tom, my plane run takes me over the desert. For some time, on moonless nights, I've seen green, red, and purple lights strung out just beyond your extra grazing lands."

This acreage was part of a ranch once owned by Bronco's father. His son had retained part of the lush pastureland near distant Fossil Mountain and used it for his cattle during dry seasons.

Mr. Davis went on, "Each time the lights have vanished suddenly, as if somebody did not want them to be seen. Does anyone live there?"

"No," Bronco replied.

"Since it's close to your fence, I thought you might want to look into it," John said.

"Thanks for the tip, Johnny. Maybe someone's helping himself to my land. I'll ride out to see what's going on."

"Oh, Bronco," Linda cried excitedly, "may Bob and I investigate with you?"

Bronco smiled and gave John a wink. "I figured I'd have two enthusiastic helpers."

John Davis advised that they not go for a few days. "Not until the moon rises late," he said. "I've noticed that unless the night is very dark the lights don't appear."

"That's strange," said Bronco. "I'll do as you say, Johnny."

At this moment, the genial Mexican housekeeper, Luisa Alvarez, appeared, bearing an antique silver tray with tall cups, a slender pot of cinnamon-spiced hot chocolate, and a silver plate of home-made cookies.

"An old family custom when callers come,"

Bronco explained. "My wife likes to use the Spanish silver."

Linda was already pouring the hot chocolate. "Doña—that has been Bob's and my nickname for Grandmother since we were very little—is out riding, or she would join us."

As soon as John Davis had finished his drink, he stood up and announced that he must leave. "Let me know how you make out."

Bob hurried off to bring Prince Brownlee, and soon the pleasant caller was waving a last farewell from far down the road.

Bronco looked into Linda's eyes and said, "I've brought news of my own. For some time, I've thought that there's no horse on Old Sol exactly right for you. While I was in town I heard of a man who has a fine young palomino for sale. How would you like to ride out to his ranch tomorrow and see it?"

"Would I!" Linda exclaimed. "Oh, Bronco, how wonderful of you!"

The rancher chuckled. "Don't praise me. Thank your grandmother. She said if I ever came across a horse especially suited to you, I was to look into the matter."

Linda's eyes became dewy. "How lucky I am to have Doña for a grandmother! She's just the grandest person in the whole world. And that goes for you, too, Bronco!"

"It sure does," Bob said with a grin.

Linda was so happy she wanted to share her good news with everyone. She ran to tell Luisa, then Cactus Mac. Both expressed delight. Next, Linda telephoned one of her best friends, Kathy Hamilton, who lived nearby.

"A palomino of your own!" Kathy cried. "Linda, how marvelous! I hope you'll find one soon."

Just before dinner time—and dinner time at Old Sol followed the Spanish custom of being late in the evening—the telephone rang. Luisa came to tell Bronco that Mr. Brownlee was calling.

After a few moments, Linda heard him exclaim, "Johnny Davis has disappeared! He's long overdue? Yes, yes, we'll go out and hunt for him pronto!"

Bronco put down the phone and called the bunkhouse. He requested Cactus Mac to saddle up his chestnut Morgan, Colonel, and go with him on the search.

Then Grandfather Mallory turned to Linda and Bob. "I'm sure you both want to be in on this," he said. "Linda, put a first-aid kit in your saddlebag. Johnny may have been thrown from his horse or had some other accident."

The Runaway 2

As Linda hurried to the tack room in the barn with Bob and Bronco, she asked, "Do you think John Davis had a natural accident?"

"What do you mean?" Bronco said, puzzled.

Linda answered slowly, "If the people who are using the strange lights he was talking about are breaking the law and knew he had reported them— well, they might have attacked him."

Bob whistled and Bronco's forehead took on a deep, worried frown. Quickly Bob remarked, "In that case, the mission we're going on in a couple of days will probably be a dangerous one."

Cactus Mac was told about the lights and insisted upon accompanying the group when they were ready to look into that mystery.

The riders strung out, Linda on roan Gypsy, Bob astride Rocket, a bay quarter horse, and Cactus Mac on Buck. The four looked intently to the left and right of the long lane that led to the main road for signs of the missing John Davis. They found a horse's hoofprints, but Johnny was not in sight.

"Ted Brownlee said he had looked all along his lane," Bronco reported, "so I'm inclined to think Johnny took a shortcut."

"Might 'a been the one that's half a mile down the road," Cactus spoke up. "Not much more'n a dry streambed, but mighty direct."

"Let's try it," Linda urged.

The heavily wooded shortcut proved to be very rocky and full of tiny but treacherous gravel pits. The riders guided their horses with constant, careful skill, pausing many times to gaze around them. There was not a sound.

Finally Linda said, "If Johnny Davis came this way, he covered a good distance. How far are we from the Brownlee ranch?"

"We're on their land," Bronco answered, "but several miles from the ranch house."

Suddenly Linda said, "Listen!"

Everyone reined up and sat motionless. From their left came a rhythmic thumping sound.

"Thar's no animal around here what makes a noise like that," Cactus Mac said, puzzled.

Instantly the riders dismounted and plunged into the woods toward the strange thumping which continued. A few seconds later Bob, in the lead, cried out, "Mr. Davis!"

The others rushed forward and saw the missing man, tightly bound and gagged, lying on the ground. He had raised his legs to pound with his boot heels against the trunk of a cottonwood.

In a flash, the rescuers had him unbound and on his feet to stretch his cramped limbs. Johnny grinned ruefully. "Hello, everybody. And thanks."

"Who did this to you?" Bronco stormed.

"A couple of your 'friendly' neighbors. Get me some water and I'll tell you the rest."

Bob dashed back to his saddlebag and brought a canteen. As Johnny drank from it, Linda tried without success to spot the show horse he had been riding. "Where's Prince Brownlee?" she asked.

"Gone! Stolen!" was the astonishing reply.

"By the men who tied you up?"

"Yes. This is what happened. When I reached a spot near here, two masked men jumped out at me from among the trees. They ordered me to get down. When I refused, they dragged me off. There was a fight—which I lost. Then the men tied me up and dragged me to this spot."

"And if you hadn't been found," said Linda indignantly, "you might have died!"

Johnny grinned at her. "Oh, I'm pretty tough!"

Bronco spoke up. "Horse thieves! They probably had a van waiting some place to haul Prince Brownlee away. Which direction did they take?"

"That's the funny part of it," Johnny said. "They led the horse on up the shortcut right toward the ranch house."

Cactus Mac, silent up to this time, snorted.

"Them hoss thieves'll prob'bly hide the Prince and try to collect a big ransom from Mr. Brownlee."

"It's a logical guess," said Bob. "I wonder how soon we'll know."

"Right now the most important thing is to get Johnny home," said Bronco. "Do you feel strong enough to ride with me on Colonel?"

"Sure." Johnny walked with the others to the horses. Bronco borrowed one of the two blankets on Linda's horse, swung it across Colonel's hips, and the two men got astride.

When the riders reached the Brownlee home, the owner and his wife rushed outside, relief showing on their faces. Linda and Bob were introduced to hearty, gray-haired Mr. Brownlee and his pleasant, slightly stout wife. Then Johnny Davis told his story.

Mr. Brownlee's face turned red with anger. "This sounds like the old West! Our peaceful community invaded by horse thieves! We'll soon stop that! I'll phone the sheriff right away!"

The group from Rancho del Sol said good-bye and hurried back to a very late dinner. Grandmother Mallory, who always insisted her family dress properly for the evening meal, awaited them in a fashionable, long-sleeved black dress. Her dark, graying hair was pulled back into a knot and held in place with a high tortoiseshell comb. She was a beautiful woman, slender and dignified, and had a warm, ready smile. Her olive skin was set off by an emerald necklace and earrings, family heirlooms. Mrs. Mallory was considered an excellent horsewoman—one of the most accomplished in the West.

"Tell me, did you find Mr. Davis?" she asked.

"Yes, Roz," Bronco replied and told the circumstances briefly.

"How unfortunate!" Grandmother Mallory said. "But at least we can be thankful he's safe now."

The searchers excused themselves and quickly changed for dinner. Conversation throughout the meal was lively. Linda felt that never in her life had so many exciting things happened to her in such a short time. The report of mysterious lights in the desert; horse thieves and the loss of a valuable show mount; and the promise of a fine palomino of her own!

Presently Bronco said, "Why don't we combine our trip to see Linda's palomino with a hunt for Prince Brownlee? Those thieves may be hiding him somewhere in the desert. We can head for Indian Charlie Tonka's cabin, which is near my grazing lands, then go on to investigate the strange lights."

"It sounds marvelous," Linda said enthusiastically. "Indian Charlie's one of the guards for the pipeline, isn't he? May I go, Doña?"

Grandmother Mallory smiled understandingly. "Of course you may go."

Linda threw her grandmother a grateful smile and said, "Thank you."

The Mallory household was up at dawn. Yet by

the time Linda reached the barn, she found Cactus Mac nearly ready to leave.

"It's rugged country we'll be riding through, and dangerous, too. Got to be well-prepared," the foreman warned.

He said that he had checked the latigo leathers on the saddles, taken down a couple of pack saddles from a shelf, and four bedrolls from a cupboard.

"And the hosses have been curried and brushed."

"Cactus, you're spoiling us!" Linda laughed. "Well, at least we can help load the packhorses."

Bob joined her and together they strapped on a small hamper of lunch, cans of food, a supply of water, a two-way radio set, the sleeping parapher-nalia, and extra clothes.

As Linda swung into her saddle, the girl's exhilaration was beyond words. Bob sat mounted and ready. Bronco was beside Linda, a .45 revolver in his gun belt. Cactus Mac carried a rifle in his saddle boot.

"For stray mountain cats or rattlesnakes," the foreman said, grinning.

With Bronco leading the way, and the two packhorses on a string behind Cactus's saddle at the rear, the ranchers rode east into the Mojave desert. Its undulating surface, dotted with cactus, juniper trees, and spiny, bent-arm Joshua trees, spread out distinctly in the clear morning sky. In the distance, wrinkled, rocky hills rose abruptly from the desert floor.

"It's beautiful!" Linda said, gazing at the scene of which she never tired. Nevertheless she was aware of the weird, weighty silence so peculiar to deserts and thought, I'll be glad to hear some whitewings cooing.

Her wish was fulfilled a moment later as two of the birds flew from a tree, giving their plaintive call, and landed on a rock to continue their song.

Bronco angled the riders' trail, and touched ranch country again. Eagerly, Linda watched for the palomino her grandfather had mentioned. She was first to see a weathered sign nailed to a fence post, announcing horses for sale.

"There are some palominos!" she cried.

As she and her companions rode up to them, Linda's spirits fell. The animals were too light in color, and one had a Roman nose, which she knew was not desirable for a show horse.

I want a palomino the color of a freshly minted gold coin, Linda thought, with a white mane and tail, and four white stockings!

The ranch owner, who was mending a fence, came to speak to Bronco. "The palomino you want to see is in the barn. I'll get him."

The horse proved to be a sleek gelding. Linda gasped. He looked exactly like her dream horse!

"How old is this palomino?" Bronco asked.

"Just going on five. Old enough to have good sense and young enough to have plenty of ginger."

"May I try him out?" Linda asked excitedly.

The rancher saddled the palomino. Linda mounted quickly, and turned out of the gate to work him on a clear spot of desert floor.

She rode around twice in a big circle. The horse had nice easy action. Then she attempted to put him through a figure eight, with little success. It took tugging to bring him about, so Linda knew he was hard-mouthed.

That toughness isn't good in a horse, she told herself.

Linda turned the palomino on a straightaway for a canter. Suddenly, he took the bit in his mouth and sped out over the desert. This was an unexpected move. Linda pulled hard on the reins, yet all her strength was not enough to stop the horse's headlong dash or even to haul him around. Going this fast, she did not dare throw herself off.

If this crazy horse keeps running, Linda thought desperately, I'll be lost in the desert!

Search in the Desert 3

Linda knew that her best hope of survival on the runaway palomino was to stick with him, praying that he would not slam a hoof into a gopher hole and throw her.

The palomino veered so sharply that Linda nearly lurched off. Then, before it could pick up speed again, her brother's lariat snaked out. The loop settled over the horse's head, bringing the animal up short.

Bob gave Linda a quick glance to be sure that she was all right, then grinned. "Nice ride?" he teased.

"Not exactly what I had in mind," she panted. "Thanks, Brother." They walked the horse back to the ranch, and Linda slid off him.

Bronco clapped Bob on the leg. "Good figuring, Bob, riding to cut them off instead of chasing straight after that horse. And a splendid catch."

"Just lucky," Bob muttered modestly.

"A fine horse," the owner said enthusiastically as

he patted the heaving palomino. "You going to buy him?"

Bronco looked into the animal's mouth, and replied curtly, "This horse's worn teeth indicate he's at least twelve years old. No, he's not the palomino for us."

"I wouldn't want him anyway," said Linda. "He's mean!"

She and Bronco and Cactus Mac mounted their horses and the four callers rode silently away from the abashed rancher. Linda was still recovering from her scare.

A short distance beyond, Bronco suggested that they stop in the shade of a few oak trees. While Linda unpacked the lunch, unable to forget her disappointment about the palomino, Bob and Cactus watered the four mounts at a little spring.

Bronco sensed the girl's mood. "Don't give up hope," he said. "We'll find just the right horse for you yet." Her answer was only a smile but it indicated the confidence she had in her grandfather.

When Linda and the men settled down under the trees to eat, Bob brandished a fried chicken leg and asked, "*This* is what you call roughing it?"

"It'll get rougher at supper time," Bronco promised him with a chuckle, "when you get your turn with a frying pan over an open fire."

After lunch, the four rode on to the mouth of a red granite canyon, where Cactus thought a horse thief could conveniently hide. As they wound along between its high walls, the shadows were deep and sounds reverberated. There was no sign of any animals.

Bronco grinned. "Kind of weird in here," he said. "Note the rock formations." He pointed out well-known ones and asked Linda, who had never been here before, to guess what they were.

"Cathedral and woman-at-an-organ," she spoke up presently. "Oh, I see an eagle, and a donkey's head!"

When they were deep in the canyon, Bronco gestured to a sloping pinnacle above them. "Bandit Rock," he said. "There's a pocket in back of it. Years ago, the famous outlaw Vasquez used to lie in wait there for people he intended to rob."

Linda felt a tingle up and down her spine. "A good place for horse thieves to hide Prince Brownlee," she remarked. "They could be up there right now, spying on us!"

"Yes," agreed Bronco. "You and Bob stay here and guard the rocks from the front. If anyone comes, yell! Cactus and I will investigate the rear."

Cautiously, the two men began to climb the slanting crags. Presently they disappeared. Linda and Bob waited with bated breath, hoping not to hear any shots to indicate a fight. None came and no strangers appeared.

Fifteen minutes later Bronco and Cactus Mac

returned. "Not a sign of Prince Brownlee," Bronco reported, "nor of any thieves."

The riders went on through the lengthening shadows. Finally they emerged from the canyon into the open, where dark, bushy junipers and sweet-smelling greasewood trees grew.

"Camping site just ahead," Bronco announced.

Soon the group reached a small ravine with a scant flow of water. After unsaddling the horses, Bob and Cactus Mac rubbed down their backs, then hobbled them so they might move about and graze.

Cactus Mac, who had never camped with Linda and Bob, watched with interest as they prepared supper. First Bob scooped out a narrow oval in the sand, built a fire in it, and rimmed it with large rocks.

On these Linda put the kettle, a skillet with bacon, and a pan of canned tomatoes. Bread and apples rounded out their supper.

"Wal, what you know? You sure can cook. The grub couldn't be better," the foreman declared, finishing the meal with a second cup of coffee.

Linda scoured their dishes with sand and paper, wiped them with a damp cloth, and put them back into the clean oat bag out of the dust.

As a big yellow moon rose over the dark, uneven skyline to the east, the weary travelers laid out their bedrolls. Bronco took a rough hemp rope from his saddle, and made a wide circle around the campers.

"What's that for?" Linda asked.

Bronco laughed. "No rattlesnake is going to crawl over that. The rope prickles its skin."

The campers pulled off their boots and slipped into the bedrolls. Linda watched the moon float higher and turn paler. Around her the bushy junipers shone like silvery ghosts. She lay awake drinking in the eerie beauty, and wondering about the mysterious lights, her dream horse, and the missing Prince Brownlee. But her eyes would not stay open long. Soon she snuggled down and went to sleep.

Linda and the others rose in the cool of the dawn. After a quick breakfast, they swung into their saddles and again looked intently for Prince Brownlee. They had no luck.

"I'm dreadfully worried about him," said Linda.

Bronco led the way to the fertile valley at the edge of which lay his grazing land. To left and right were majestic mountains.

Mr. Mallory and his grandchildren looked in every direction. There was no sign of a person, cattle, horses, or any type of equipment for lighting up the area. Finally the riders went on.

"We may be able to see the strange lights from Charlie's," Bronco remarked. "Then we'll know where to look for them."

It was mid-afternoon when they arrived, hot and tired, at the top of the mountain to the left, where

Indian Charlie lived. Under the shade of planted acacia and elderberry trees, they saw his log cabin. On the far side of it stood a shed barn. Between the buildings was a corral.

Linda suddenly straightened in the saddle, reined up, and pointed at the enclosure. "Look!" she cried.

Inside was a little palomino filly daintily prancing in excitement at the visitors' approach. The graceful creature, tossing its white mane and tail, trotted to the fence and whinnied.

"Oh!" Linda breathed softly, unable to say more. "Oh, oh, oh!" she repeated in delight. Swiftly she jumped from the saddle and ran to get a closer look. "Gold!" the excited girl exclaimed happily. "Pure gold, and four white stockings!"

Bronco, Bob, and Cactus Mac exchanged grins. As they dismounted, Charlie Tonka came running from the cabin.

"Señor Bronco! Señor Bronco!" he exclaimed, and flung his arms around the big man.

"What luck to find you at home!" Bronco said smiling, and shook the Indian's hand. "You know Cactus Mac. I'd like you to meet my grandchildren," he added proudly. "Linda and Bob Craig."

Hearing her name, Linda pulled herself away from the palomino and joined the men. Charlie grasped her hand, then Bob's in welcome. The Indian was lean and bony, and the tight skin of his face shone like polished copper. His black hair, with a little gray in it, was brushed straight back and cut square across the nape of his neck.

"Can you stay long?" Charlie asked, beaming.

"As long as we need to clear up a little mystery."

"Ah, good!" said Charlie. "What do you want to solve?"

Bronco told about the strange lights near his grazing grounds. "Have you ever seen them?"

"Lights? Near your grazing fields? No, Señor Bronco. You think there is funny business going on?"

"We don't know exactly."

The horses were taken care of and turned into the section of the corral where Charlie's black Tennessee walker, Jim, welcomed them with nosing and nickering. Then Bob and Cactus carried the visitors' belongings into the cabin.

Linda yearned to stay with the little filly, but went along. I wonder if the palomino could possibly be for sale, she asked herself.

The interior of the cabin was rectangularly shaped—clean, neat, and bare. Cots flanked each long wall. There was a gas cookstove and cupboards at the far end of the room. In the center was a plain wooden table and four chairs.

"I'll have my own bed out under the stars," Cactus Mac announced.

The other end of the room had been partitioned off into a narrow section for storage of provisions.

"Linda, you sleep with the food," Charlie said,

grinning, and dragged one of the beds into this section.

As soon as Linda had set her bundle of clothing beside her bed, she slipped outdoors and hurried to the corral. Quietly she opened the gate and stepped inside.

The filly raised her head. Linda stood still. For a moment the two looked at each other. Then the palomino snorted lightly and shifted uneasily. Linda walked toward her, talking softly, and in a moment laid her hand on the silky, golden nose. Unknown to Linda, the men had followed and were watching her over the fence.

"You like my young'un?" Charlie asked, coming into the enclosure.

Linda's heart sank as she saw him gently stroke the horse's mane. She felt sure he would never want to part with his pet.

"Where did you get her?" Linda asked.

"One day I found her mother in the brush. She was a fine sorrel Arabian," Charlie informed the girl. "She was badly torn by wild animals. I brought her to the corral. She foaled this little golden filly. In a few days, the mother died. I fed young'un with a bottle. She is over two years old now."

The Indian chuckled. "Young'un very smart. Too smart sometimes. She slides the bolt on the gate." He squinted his eyes. "I think maybe her mother did the same thing. That is how she wandered off and got lost."

Charlie went on, "Her little one learns fast. Watch this." The Indian said "How!" and the filly raised her dainty right foreleg to "shake hands."

"Oh, you darling!" Linda cried softly, wrapping her arms about the golden neck. "I wish you were mine, you lovely creature!" Then she laughed. "If you were mine, I'd call you—well, I'd call you Chica d'Oro—little girl of gold!"

"That's a good name," Charlie agreed. "You call her that." But he did not say a word about selling the pony to Linda.

The next morning the Indian set off on his duties as guard for the cross-country gas pipeline. He planned to stay that night in a hut at the other end of the range.

"You make yourselves at home," he called from the walker's back as he rode off.

Bronco gave Linda a steady gaze, then asked, "Do you want to stay here while Cactus, Bob, and I scout around for some clue to the mysterious lights? Or would you rather come along?"

Linda was torn between two desires—helping to solve the mystery, and trying to teach the palomino a trick.

Her grandfather, guessing that she wanted to work with the pony, answered the question for the undecided girl. "If there's a horse thief around, that palomino ought to be protected, I suppose. Tell you what, Linda. See that bell on the post? If there's any trouble, ring that, and we'll come running."

"All right," Linda agreed, happy at the arrangement.

In a few minutes, she was alone. Taking several slices of bread in her hand, Linda hurried eagerly to the corral. Chica d'Oro promptly trotted over to her. The filly was used to having Charlie give her pieces of bread for a treat. Linda broke off one corner of a slice and put it in the pocket of her shirt. The palomino tried to pull it out with her soft lips.

"Good girl," Linda praised her.

Linda wrapped the bread in her handkerchief, tucked it in the pocket with the corner dangling, and Chica pulled it out. Soon the horse was pulling the handkerchief out whether there was bread in it or not.

"Oh, you wonderful pony!" Linda said affectionately.

When Bronco and Bob rode in at noon with Cactus Mac, she had them watch the trick.

"That horse has sense," Bronco said in praise.

Bob told his sister that they had found nothing in the area of his grandfather's grazing land to indicate any trespasser—the fences were intact. But as soon as the four had eaten, the men took off again on a more extensive search for a clue to the mysterious lights. Linda began clearing the table in a hurry so she could get back to Chica d'Oro.

Suddenly she heard the filly begin to prance and whinny shrilly. Dropping the spoons she held, Linda ran outside and was almost to the corral fence when she stopped short. A harsh, dry rattling sound was coming from the enclosure.

A rattler—a deadly rattler! Linda thought in terror. Chica d'Oro's in danger!

Trembling, she forced herself to walk quietly to the gate and look over it. In front of the distraught pony was coiled a big diamondback, its head erect and its tail warning of an attack.

Linda froze. If Chica strikes at the snake, it'll bite her! The pony might die!

Burro Trap 4

Quick as lightning, Linda grabbed a sharp rock near
her feet and hurled it with all her strength at the
rattler. The stone hit, but rolled off. The reptile had
been hurt, however. It recoiled and started to
slither out of the corral. Linda ran for a shovel she
saw leaning against the barn. Hurrying up behind
the snake, she ended its life with one blow.

Oh, Chica d'Oro, you're safe! she thought in
relief.

For a moment the girl leaned weakly against the
fence. Then, knowing the poisonous snake should
not be left around, she swiftly scooped the dead
reptile up in the shovel and buried it among some
nearby bushes.

Too bad that had to be done, Linda thought.
Rattlers have their use keeping down rodents. But
right now I'd prefer a rat!

Finally she went into the corral and petted the
palomino, whose chest was heaving from fright.

"What a scare!" Linda said. "You poor thing!"

When Chica d'Oro was calm again, Linda talked to her for a long time. The pony responded with nuzzles and head shakes. "I'm pretty crazy about you," the girl said excitedly. "Oh, what can I do to make Indian Charlie sell you to me?"

When Bronco, Bob, and Cactus Mac returned, she told them about the rattler and they praised her quick thinking. Bob, noticing that his sister was still shaken, and hoping to tease her into smiling again, offered to bring her the rattles from the snake.

"No, thank you!" Linda stated positively. Then seeing the twinkle in his eyes, she added, "Okay, Brother, I get it. But don't you dare dig up that beast!"

"You do not want your trophy? Now what do you think of that, Señor Bronco?" Cactus Mac asked, imitating Indian Charlie. At this they all burst into laughter, and Linda felt better.

"Tell me about your trip," she urged the men. "Did you learn anything about the lights or about Prince Brownlee?"

"No, sorry to say," Bronco replied. "We'll look again tomorrow."

The next day brought no better results. Early that evening, Bronco put Chica d'Oro in the barn away from snakes and marauding animals and Linda joined the men in a short ride to meet Indian Charlie. It was dusk when they saw him in the distance and spurred toward the Indian.

As they drew close and reined up, Linda exclaimed, "Look!" She pointed down to her right. "Hoofprints!" As they all scanned the ground, she added, "They're only in one place, though. How could that be?"

Bronco had a ready explanation. The horse had been ridden to the spot over an outcropping of smooth rocks that extended for some distance then disappeared into a woods.

"Pretty hard on the poor horse," Linda said sympathetically.

A moment later Charlie caught up to them. He dismounted and examined the ground. "Fresh print," he told them. "Made sometime today."

There was speculation as to whether or not an innocent rider had been in the locale, or perhaps the rider was one of the horse thieves.

"The horse *could* have been Prince Brownlee," Linda suggested.

She and the others made a search of the area but did not find the missing show horse. No one was around, and finally they went back to Indian Charlie's cabin.

After supper, the group walked out onto the grassy promontory beyond the cabin from which, by daylight, they could survey the ranches and valley for miles around. Silhouettes of trees and bushes stood out like black ghosts. Suddenly, in the distance, several varicolored lights flashed on.

"They must be some of the lights John Davis was

talking about!" Linda exclaimed tensely. "Oh, Charlie, is there any way we can get down the mountain and find out?"

"No good at night. You would break a leg. Go tomorrow with horses. I have a couple days off—I will come with you."

Linda felt impatient at the delay, but could do nothing except wait. She and her companions tried to place the exact spot of the strange sight. Charlie gave a clue. "The lights are on the other side of the valley at the edge of Fossil Mountain. You will find it easy."

An hour later the lights, which had blinked on and off intermittently, vanished completely.

"We'd better get some sleep," Bronco said, yawning.

In the morning, Cactus Mac elected to stay at the cabin, while the others rode off to find the lights. This time Bob brought up the rear. Linda was just ahead, calling back speculations about what they would find.

It suddenly occurred to her that Bob was not replying. She turned in her saddle and gave a gasp. Her brother and his mount had disappeared from sight! It was as if they had been swallowed up by the earth!

She heard a muffled cry and thought in terror, Bob's been hurt!

With a sharp sense of danger, she reined Gypsy back. Suppose Bob were in trouble greater than she could cope with? She spun around, at the same time shouting frantically, "Bronco! Charlie!"

At Linda's outcry, the two men stopped abruptly and galloped back to her.

"Something has happened to Bob!" she exclaimed, pointing to where he had been. "He's gone!"

They all made for the spot, and came to the edge of an oblong pit that had been covered over with brush.

"Help!" came a plea from below. "Rocket broke through!"

With a leap Linda, Bronco, and Indian Charlie were off their mounts and leaning over the edge of the opening.

"Bob, are you all right?" Linda called down frantically.

They could dimly see the horse, but Bob was not in the saddle. "Yes, I'm all right. Just examining Rocket's legs."

"Is he hurt?" Linda asked anxiously.

"Don't think so," Bob replied. "One leg may be sprained some. But how are we going to get him out of here?"

"We will get you out," Charlie shouted. "I will go to the cabin for a spade."

"Who made this trap here—and why?" Linda asked, perplexed.

"Some tinhorn fixed it up to catch a wild burro," Bronco replied, angrily kicking aside the brush. "It would never catch a burro—they're too smart. But it could kill a rider!"

Linda did not comment. She wondered if the trap might have been made for some other reason. Perhaps by the horse thieves or even the people with mysterious lights.

As soon as Charlie returned, he energetically began scraping away the salty earth at one end of the pit. Bronco spelled him, and shortly they had made a steep incline.

The rancher threw down one end of his rope to Bob and called instructions. "Fix a loop around Rocket's rump and mount up. When you hear me yell, boot him out of there."

Bronco now fastened his end of the rope to his saddlehorn, swung onto Colonel's back, gave a yell, and sent the horse hard ahead, away from the pit.

When Rocket felt the tightening rope around his rump, it annoyed him. With Bob's boot heel urging him on, he decided to come up the steep ramp in leaps and bounds.

"Whew!" exclaimed Bob. "That's the roughest ride I ever had. And I guess I'll have to give up the trip. Rocket's limping."

"We'll all go back," Bronco declared.

Charlie filled the pit with loose boughs and brush. Then the four sleuths started for his cabin, with Bob walking beside Rocket.

Once back there, the Indian gave Bob a bottle of liniment which he applied to Rocket's sprained leg.

The following morning it seemed slightly improved and Bob again rubbed the leg with liniment.

"He will be good as new in two days," Charlie assured him. "Then we will make the trip to the lights."

Again Linda was sorry for the delay but she decided in the interim to give her attention to Chica d'Oro and went to the corral. Running her hand lovingly over the palomino's mane, she murmured to it caressingly.

"You like my little young'un, eh?" Charlie beamed.

"More than any animal I've ever known," replied Linda earnestly. Then she asked, "Is Chica broken to the saddle?"

"No, but last month I broke her to hackamore," Charlie answered.

Linda was pleased. The hackamore's gentler than a bridle, she thought. It's constructed the same, except it has no bit. The bosal, which passed through the cheek straps, Linda knew, effected control.

"Would you like to ride her around the corral?" Charlie asked. "It would be good for her."

"I'd love to," Linda said excitedly.

Charlie went to the barn for the trappings. When he returned, Linda noted with relief that the braided rawhide bosal was well padded underneath. It was brought to a knot under the chin, and finished with a red tassel.

She chuckled. "It looks cute on Chica d'Oro—she's so dainty."

Charlie smoothed an Indian blanket over the horse's back and fastened it on with a surcingle. This leather band, which went around the horse, had a leather hand grip on top, and a couple of dangling stirrups.

"You ride all right like this?" Charlie asked Linda.

She nodded. "I've been riding around the ranch bareback. Takes less time to jump on that way than to saddle up," she added, laughing, and pulled herself easily onto Chica d'Oro's back.

The palomino danced sideways, but Linda gathered her in with the reins, and got her to heading straight in a few moments. Chica d'Oro was coltish and green, but settled down more and more to Linda's gentle guidance.

The pony began to respond nicely. Soon she was turning promptly in the direction indicated by the touch of the rein on her neck.

Not wanting Chica d'Oro to become nervous or jumpy from too prolonged a workout, Linda stopped her at the barn in about thirty minutes. She removed the trappings, and with a piece of clean sacking, rubbed down the pony's golden back until it shone.

"You're such a beauty," the girl said admiringly.

Late that afternoon Linda, Bob, and Bronco were leaning on the corral fence absorbed in watching

Charlie and Cactus Mac, who were in the enclosure.

Presently Bronco said, "I remember, Charlie, the times you and Cactus Mac put on that stunt of yours at some ranch rodeo. You'd send the bunch into stitches. How about showing it to Linda and Bob?"

"Oh, please do," Linda begged.

"We-ell now, I don't know about that." Cactus hesitated. "How about you, Charlie? You as spry as ever?"

Charlie straightened. "I am spry," he replied with offended dignity. "I will get the smoke bomb."

He hurried into the kitchen and returned with a large pan of flour. Cactus Mac had saddled up and mounted his horse Buck. Now he took the pan and announced in a barker's stagey voice, "Lady and gentlemen, I be introducin' the great humbug, Perfessor Galoot, and Chief Hog-Um-Gold."

Linda and Bob burst into laughter, then watched in fascination as the act began. Charlie, on foot, pretended to run off to the corral gate. Cactus promptly lassoed the Indian and brought him back.

"Tell me whar that there rich vein o' gold is located in yonder old Humpy Mountain, or you die!" proclaimed Cactus.

"I not tell," growled Charlie. "I not die."

"Perfessor Galoot" loosened the rope from Charlie, and started riding about in a close circle. "You tell or sure as shootin' I'll call on many demons to skin you alive!"

"I no tell. You no know demons."

"You tell or I'll make you disappear."

"I no tell. I no disappear."

"Ho!" shouted Cactus Mac, riding around Charlie faster. "Yippee-ki-oo, and a good-bye to you!"

Then he slammed the pan of flour in front of Charlie, and galloped to one side. When the white cloud subsided, Charlie was gone!

"What happened to him?" Linda cried in real amazement.

Bob stared with an astounded grin. "That's a real disappearing act, if ever I saw one!"

"But where is he?" asked Linda.

"Maybe he went through a trapdoor into the ground," Bronco suggested. "Cactus, you'd better make Charlie reappear in a hurry, or you'll have to ride herd on his pipeline."

As the foreman from Rancho del Sol grinned, Charlie dropped to the ground from the far side of Buck. He had leaped there, grasped the stirrup leather with both hands, and had been holding his body parallel to that of the animal.

The Craigs applauded and howled with laughter. Then Bob said, "That's a great trick. The only one I know with flour is making a cake disappear!"

For hours after supper, the group watched for the strange lights across the valley. But they were not turned on.

After breakfast next day, Charlie asked the men to go with him on an inspection trip. They also would keep a sharp lookout for clues to Prince Brownlee. "You take care of the young'un?" the Indian asked Linda. "She is in the corral."

"Indeed, I will," she answered, delighted at the thought.

As Linda tidied the cabin, she heard the palomino whinny shrilly. The girl froze. The horse's cry was not one of terror as at the snake. It showed the nervous excitement Chica d'Oro had displayed when the visitors from Rancho del Sol had first ridden up to the corral.

There must be a caller, Linda thought.

She clenched her hands tensely. Who was out there? The horse thieves? With a knot in her throat, she ran to the window and peered into the yard.

The Fossil Clue 5

Linda gasped at the sight of an unshaven, dusty rider by the corral. She stood frozen, watching and hoping that he would ride away.

But when he dismounted with an old rope halter and tie rope in his hand, and started to open the corral gate, Linda rushed out. He's going to steal Chica! she thought in dismay.

The man stopped and regarded the girl in surprise. It was apparent that he had thought nobody was on the place.

"What are you doing here?" Linda demanded. "What do you want? What's your name?"

"Luke Poe," the man said in a slurred tone. "I'm a friend of Charlie Tonka's. I take care of his horse when he's gone."

Linda was speechless for a few moments, thinking it odd that Charlie had not mentioned this. She was sure that the Indian had said he always put the palomino in the stall with plenty of food and water when he went away.

Now the man asked curiously, "Who're you?"

"I'm visiting here with a group from Rancho del Sol," Linda replied coolly.

"Where's everybody else?" he inquired.

"They'll be back any second," she said and decided she had better run and ring the alarm bell. But she changed her mind as Luke Poe, with a sneering smile, pushed open the corral gate and went inside.

"I'll take the horse out for some exercise," he said boldly.

As he entered the corral, Chica d'Oro danced back and forth, nickering uncertainly. When Luke Poe reached up to put the dirty rope halter on her, she pranced away from him.

"Come here, you!" he said roughly, and jumped after the pony.

He threw the end of the tie rope over Chica's neck to hold her, and quickly slipped on the halter. He fastened it, then started to lead the palomino out of the corral.

Instantly Linda slammed the gate shut. "You're not taking that horse out of here!"

"Get out of my way, girl!" the man ordered. Reaching through the rails of the fence, he pushed Linda so hard that she fell to the ground.

He mustn't steal Chica d'Oro! Linda thought in panic.

Suddenly, as Luke started to open the gate, Chica d'Oro reared with a high squeal, striking at the man with her hooves and pulling the rope from his hand. He grabbed for it with one hand, while attempting to pull open the gate with the other.

The palomino rose up on her hind legs again and once more went at Luke with her flailing front hooves. One of them struck his arm, tearing the sleeve of his coat.

Linda jumped to her feet and cried, "She'll kill you!"

As Chica d'Oro went up in the air again, a look of terror flashed across Luke Poe's face. He quickly clambered over the rails, jumped on his horse, and galloped away.

Linda calmed down at once. She leaned over the fence, saying, "Everything's okay, young'un. Don't be frightened any more. You and I had a good scare, but that horrid man is gone."

Nevertheless, it was ten minutes before Linda felt it was wise to enter the corral. Then she hugged Chica d'Oro, pressing her cheek against one side of the palomino's head. The pony nickered softly as Linda took off the halter.

On the ground lay a handkerchief. Luke must have dropped it, Linda decided.

Realizing she should keep it as a possible clue to the man's identity, if he had given a false name, Linda picked it up. Then she noticed something which lay beneath it—a hard, round, slightly concave shell.

Luke must have dropped this, too! she thought.

After another reassuring pat for the palomino, Linda took the two clues into the cabin and put them on a shelf. All this time she was mulling over several ideas. "Perhaps Poe knew Chica d'Oro's Arabian mother! He traced her colt here to Charlie's and waited for a chance to steal her! Maybe he's even one of the men who took Prince Brownlee!"

Linda went out to feed the filly, then returned to the cabin and started supper. In a little while, the men returned.

At once, Charlie asked, "Who has been here? There are strange horse tracks outside."

Linda told them of Luke Poe and his rough actions.

"I know nobody by that name," Charlie declared. "I did not hire him or anyone else to take care of young'un."

"This must be reported at once," Bronco declared.

He tuned in their two-way radio to Rancho del Sol and talked to Grandmother Mallory. After learning that affairs were running fairly well at the ranch, he asked his wife to report the attempted theft to the sheriff.

"Linda will give you the man's description," he said. "She had a good look at the fellow."

"Oh, Linda dear," her grandmother said, after hearing the story, "this must mean you were in great danger. Perhaps you should come home?"

Linda laughed. "The scare is over, Doña. And I must stay here to help solve the mystery of those queer lights. We've spotted their location."

Mrs. Mallory begged her granddaughter to be careful.

"I will," Linda promised and chuckling, added, "I'll tell Bob and Bronco to watch their step, too!"

After the conversation was finished, Linda showed the men the handkerchief and shell she had picked up in the corral. Charlie examined the articles with interest.

"This ancient clam shell is from Fossil Mountain over there," he informed them. "High, jagged. It is full of old shells. Smart men say thousands of years ago it rose up out of the ocean."

"I'm familiar with that peak," said Bronco. "The rocky soil is crumbly and treacherous to travel on in some places."

Cactus Mac spoke up. "Pokin' around, it's dangerous business, sure enough."

"If that's true, not many people would be prowling around there," Bob observed. "It would be a good place for a hideout."

"And if Poe came from there, then he probably is in hiding," Linda guessed.

"Very possibly," Bronco agreed.

"That fellow left a good trail when he took off,"

said Bob. "How about our riding out tomorrow morning, Linda, to see how far we can follow it? Rocket's okay now."

"Yes, let's," she replied eagerly. "We might even find that Luke has Prince Brownlee there! I'll pack a lunch in case we get hungry."

"Good luck!" said Bronco. "And promise me you won't try to make a capture alone. Come back to report it over the radio if you see this Luke Poe."

Linda promised, then said, "In the meantime, you take good care of Chica d'Oro." She wagged her finger playfully.

The men looked at one another guiltily, then Bronco admitted they had all planned to ride off. "Mac's going back to the ranch, and since Charlie needs a little help on the pipeline, I was going with him."

Linda's forehead puckered. "But we can't *all* go. We don't dare leave the palomino."

"I will put padlocks on the corral gate and stall door," Charlie offered.

"Those wouldn't do a bit of good if anyone is determined to steal Chica d'Oro," Linda said worriedly. "The thief would break in."

"You're right," agreed Bronco.

"I know of one solution," Linda offered brightly. "If you wouldn't mind, Charlie, I could ride Chica d'Oro."

"Sure, why not?" Bob asked. "Since apparently it's only the palomino someone wants to steal, the other horses, which are branded, won't be bothered."

The Indian grinned. "Okay, Linda. You ride the young'un. But she has no shoes. It will break the edges of her hooves to walk on pebbles."

Linda was crestfallen. "And there is no blacksmith anywhere around, is there?"

Charlie saw her disappointed expression. "I will put on shoes," he said quickly. "I will do it now."

"Oh, wonderful!" Linda exclaimed, happy again. "Is there anything you can't do, Charlie?"

"I did not find who has those funny lights in desert," he answered. "Maybe bad people."

"Don't worry. We'll solve the mystery," Linda assured him.

Charlie took the bright gasoline lantern from its hook in the ceiling and went out to the barn, trailed by the others.

"Where are your forge and anvil?" Bob asked.

"I do not have any," answered the Indian. "I shoe cold."

"I didn't know that was possible," said Linda, surprised.

"It's the way cowboys do it on the range," Bronco informed her. "They either shoe that way or they're likely to find themselves afoot or with a permanently lame horse."

Charlie went about gathering together different sizes of iron horseshoes, nails, knife, clippers, and a rasp. He said to Linda, "You get young'un."

Chica d'Oro had been put in her stall for the night. Linda haltered her, then led the horse into the center of the barn.

Charlie had been keeping her feet trimmed, so she promptly lifted a hoof for him to fix now. As he worked, Linda stood at Chica d'Oro's head, holding the halter rope and talking to her. The palomino nuzzled the girl and made no fuss while Charlie fitted the correct size of horsehoe to her hoof and nailed it on.

Bob watched every move intently, praised Charlie, and said to Linda, "You sure have a way with horses."

When the job was completed, Charlie said, "Turn young'un loose in the corral so she will get used to shoes."

Linda did so, and Chica d'Oro danced coltishly off into the enclosure. Finally she settled down to the feel of her iron shoes, and started walking about, bending her knees and picking her feet up high.

"Look at her, Bronco!" Linda gasped. "She's just like a full-fledged parade horse!"

Silently the girl pleaded, *Charlie, please, please let me have Chica d'Oro for my very own.* But there was a big ache in her chest because she felt sure he would never do it.

Linda managed to shake off the mood when Bob asked her to walk out onto the promontory and look for the mysterious lights. They did not appear and two hours later he said with a yawn, "John Davis told us the lights came on only when it was very dark. But maybe not on all dark nights."

Early the next morning Linda rushed out to the barn to see Chica d'Oro, who was chomping on her breakfast hay. Charlie and Bronco had gone out earlier to feed all the horses.

Linda held up the hackamore for the palomino to see. "Do you want to go on a long ride today? Some-place you've never been before?"

Chica d'Oro threw her head back and whinnied.

"You do know what I say to you, don't you?" Linda asked her softly.

The pony whinnied again through a mouthful of hay.

"Horses like to be talked to," Charlie said, walking over to Linda. "They know what you mean by the sound of your voice. You ask a question, it is instinct to try to answer. You give a command, a horse stands at attention. She wants to please." He laid a fond hand on the palomino's rump. "If a person acts mean like Luke Poe, the horse feels mean, too. Strikes with hoofs. You saw yourself."

Linda nodded. "Now we'd better go in and eat our breakfast, Charlie. Bob is fixing it. And I have lunches to pack."

"You spoil me." Charlie grinned. "How am I ever going to like dry bread for lunch again?"

"I'm glad you're spoiled," Linda answered, smiling, as they went into the house.

Bob, with a dish towel tucked around his middle,

was spooning rounds of pancake batter onto one griddle, and turning bacon on another. Bronco and Cactus were already eating. Linda and Charlie joined them, followed by the cook.

When they had finished, Cactus Mac rode off. The other men tidied the cabin while Linda prepared a stack of sandwiches from canned meat. She made four oblong packages of sandwiches, brownies, and prunes, and wrapped each in a clean piece of tarp for tying behind the cantles of the saddles.

Since she could carry nothing on a surcingle, she had packaged her food with Bob's. Next she filled the four canteens with water, to be swung from saddle strings. Charlie and Bronco carried the lunches and other gear out to the horses.

Before leaving, Linda tied a new red bandanna around her neck, and tossed a blue one to Bob. The neckerchiefs would serve to pull up over their faces as protection from stinging sand in case of a windstorm.

Bob fastened a hunting knife in a leather scabbard to his belt. Then, grabbing a lariat to hang over the pommel of his saddle, he strode out the door behind Linda.

Charlie and Bronco were ready to go and waved good-bye. The latter cautioned Bob and Linda.

"Just follow the tracks. Don't get into a tangle with any ruffian. Come back here and radio for help."

"I hope we learn where Luke Poe hangs out, and what he's up to," Bob said. Then he grinned. "Don't worry about us."

Chica d'Oro was so excited and fidgety that Linda had difficulty getting the surcingle fastened firmly. The palomino managed to dance close enough to Rocket to reach out and flutter her lips along his neck. The older horse stood still, and gave the flighty young animal a tolerant side look from soft, wise eyes.

When Bob and Linda started off, they found it was easy to follow Luke Poe's trail. It led directly toward Fossil Mountain.

"Just as we thought," said Bob. "And we have Chica to thank for the clam shell clue, giddy equine though she may be."

With a tender laugh, Linda reached out to pat the filly's neck. "Don't you pay a bit of attention to him, baby," she cooed. "He's only kidding."

Chica d'Oro apparently did not mind the aspersion. She minced along gaily, mostly concerned with keeping nose to nose with Bob's mount.

"Speaking of clues," Linda went on, "do you think there is any connection between the horse thieves who took Prince Brownlee, and Luke Poe?"

"Could be," her brother replied slowly.

The hemmed-in valley had begun to shimmer with heat, and the riders were relieved when Poe's trail led into a shady gap in the mountain. The chaparral growth on the side walls was grayish green, and the erosion patterns were like rippled satin. Many little ravines branched off from the trail Poe had taken, filled with lush undergrowth dotted with red Indian paintbrush. Apricot mallow grew riotously in spots.

"There must be water near the surface here," Bob commented.

"But it doesn't last all the way to the top," Linda remarked, noting the small pines scattered here and there far above them. "Where do you suppose the fossils are, Bob?"

"On the peak above the timber," he replied. "We'll take a good look at it, but won't risk riding up."

Suddenly a young deer bounded into their path and stopped still in surprise. Startled, Rocket jumped to one side. Chica d'Oro reared, then bolted off like a shot!

When Linda finally pulled her in among a dense flat of pines, she spoke to the palomino in a low, quieting tone. "You're all right, golden girl. That was only a little deer, and a deer never hurt anyone." She stroked the pony soothingly along the neck.

When Chica d'Oro's quivering subsided, Linda said, "Come on now, let's get back to Bob," and gave the pony a flick with the reins. At this, the filly balked.

"Oh, come on now," Linda urged. "You have to learn to be a good trail horse." The palomino still stood stiff-legged. Linda clicked the animal's sides with her heels. Finally, Chica d'Oro resentfully dogged ahead among the trees.

"That's the girl," Linda said.

In a few minutes, she was sure they were not going in the right direction. They were riding deeper into the woods instead of toward the trail where Bob was waiting. Linda felt panicky. She was lost on Fossil Mountain!

No Trespassing 6

Linda reined up and sat still to think. Which way should she go?

I mustn't panic, the young rider told herself. Then a sudden thought came to her and she leaned forward to caress Chica d'Oro.

"You knew this was the wrong way, didn't you?" she said. "And I wouldn't pay any attention to you."

Linda turned the palomino around, and gave the pony her head. But she did not move. With a sinking sensation, the girl realized Chica d'Oro did not have the slightest idea which way to go.

Sharply Linda called, "Bob! Bob!" But her voice did not seem to reach far. Worse yet, if her brother had come looking for her, he might have taken a different course through the dense pines. She would have left no trail on the soft carpet of dry needles.

"Well, let's head out this opposite way," Linda said to the pony, and urged her on.

But Chica d'Oro stopped so abruptly that Linda nearly sailed over the palomino's head. Her ears were pricked forward. Linda heard a noise in the underbrush.

She tensed and her heart pounded. Was someone hiding there? Luke Poe, maybe? Had he been following her and was now waiting in ambush? Linda sat still and strained to listen. A large bird rose from the brush and winged away.

Linda laughed softly. "Chica, you'll have to get used to such things." Then she called again, "Bob! Bob!"

Her hands tightened on the reins, and her fear of being lost was imparted to the horse. Chica d'Oro began prancing in one spot.

Instantly Linda released the reins, and with studied control pressed a hand on the pony's neck. "Quiet, baby," she said. "Someone will find us eventually."

Eventually! Not for days, maybe! If anything happened to Charlie's "young'un," Linda was sure the Indian would never forgive her. And she would never forgive herself.

Under her steadying hand, the palomino had settled down. In fact, the filly seemed to be enjoying herself here among the pines. She held her head high, moving it about, and seemed to be pleasurably sniffing the aromatic scent.

Then, on her own, the horse started trotting confidently in another direction. Linda was amazed, but figured that the animal had picked up a familiar scent—perhaps Rocket's—and she let Chica d'Oro go on weaving among the pines.

In a few minutes, through an opening among the trees, Linda caught a glimpse of the trail. The palomino turned toward it, and found her way down through the ravine. She emerged at the spot where Bob sat waiting on his horse, concern on his face.

"What were you two doing?" he asked.

"I was lost," Linda admitted sheepishly. "But Chica knew the way."

"Horse sense," Bob commented. "And *you* have been trying to teach *her* tricks!"

"Just the same," Linda declared, "I am going to buy a compass to carry when I'm riding."

"That goes double," Bob agreed. He squinted up at the sun. "Almost noon," he said.

"What do we do now?" asked Linda.

"Well, we lost Poe's trail," he replied. "It doesn't show up on this tufty rock floor. The scoundrel could be holed up anywhere in this wilderness. We might just as well keep riding, and see what we can discover."

They rode on among the trees, catching glimpses of the valley and the mountain opposite where Indian Charlie lived. At one point, they forded a narrow creek that tumbled down the steep slope.

A little farther along Linda pointed. Nestled among the trees part way up the side of Fossil

Mountain was a large rustic building of split logs that might have been a lodge or a hotel.

"Do you suppose that could be where Luke Poe lives?" Linda asked. "And look! Hoof marks! The same as the ones we were following!"

"Yes," Bob agreed. "But right now there isn't a horse in sight. Let's scout around!"

He and his sister eased their way down the mountainside in a zigzag manner to keep from slipping.

"I think Chica d'Oro is getting tired," Linda remarked. "It'll be good to give her a rest."

"We'll shade up over by that log building and eat our lunch," Bob replied.

"And keep our eyes open!" Linda added.

A short distance from the lodge stood another building, a large, gray, frame structure built against the mountain. Over the door was a sign: MINERAL SPRINGS BOTTLING CO.

"I guess this must have been the office for a health resort," Linda suggested absently, noting that there were hoofprints crossing and recrossing the area. "I wonder why a lot of horses have been here lately."

Bob shrugged. "Now don't tell me some of these prints belong to Prince Brownlee!" He went on, "A drink of that mineral water would taste good right now. Let's see if there's a spring around back."

They dismounted and Bob told Linda, "Wrap Chica's reins around my saddlehorn. Rocket ground-hitches." He dropped the bay's reins to the earth.

As Linda and Bob started forward, the office door was flung open, and two middle-aged men stepped out. They were well-dressed and clean shaven, but had a glowering manner.

"Get out, you snoopers!" commanded one, and the other said harshly, "This is private property!"

Bob and Linda stood speechless. Finally Bob bristled and was about to speak when Linda touched his arm. It had occurred to her they might learn something about the horse thief if they showed no resentment.

Quickly Linda said, "We're sorry. We didn't mean to trespass."

Bob controlled his anger and said firmly but politely, "We thought the place was deserted. Otherwise we'd have asked permission to get a drink of your mineral water."

"We planned to eat our lunch here." Linda pointed toward the log building. "Under those nice shade trees. We didn't mean any harm," she assured the men gently.

They were taken aback and exchanged quick glances. Then the taller one said with forced affability, "If we spoke a little rough it's because we've had prowlers. We don't want anyone breaking in here and causing damage."

"Oh, we understand," Linda replied. "There's been a prowler, too, at the cabin where we're staying. His trail led toward this mountain. Maybe he's the same one who has been bothering you."

The other man, a squat, powerful fellow, spoke up. "What did he look like?" he asked, squinting steadily at Linda.

"He was medium in height and thin," she answered, "and had a brown, fuzzy stubble on his face. He was poorly dressed."

"That description fits the fellow we've seen around here," the man said.

"And did his horse leave all these hoofprints?" Linda asked, trying to sound naïve.

The other one nodded, then turned toward the frame building. "Well, since it is only a drink of water you want, come on in."

Linda and Bob followed the man into a room furnished with a couple of pine desks, two plain wooden chairs, a faded-looking daybed, and a small wood-burning stove in one corner. A bottle of water stood on one desk, with a tin cup beside it.

In the back wall was a wide sliding door. It was open, revealing a large yard in the rear, between the building and the mountain. In it stood several big glass demijohns, crates, and a pickup truck for hauling the bottled water away.

"We're Bob and Linda Craig from the Rancho del Sol in the San Quinto Valley," Bob said.

The taller man cleared his throat and said in return, "I'm Worley, and this is my partner, Mr. Garrant." Then he poured out a cup of water and handed it to Linda. She sipped it experimentally, and exclaimed, "Why, this is good!"

While Bob was drinking his cup of water, Linda stood at the wide open door and looked up the side of the mountain into the dark, yawning mouth of a cave.

"My goodness!" she exclaimed. "Do some sort of wild animals live up there?"

Bob joined her, looking about intently.

"No animals," Mr. Garrant said with a small, clipped laugh. "That's where the mineral springs are."

"Thank you," said Bob, putting down the cup. "We appreciate this. If you have no objections, we'd like to eat our lunch by that log building. Then we'll ride on."

"Go ahead," Garrant said.

Mr. Worley put in hastily, "If you two young folks would like to try a shortcut out, I can show you one."

"That would be a good idea," Linda said, "My horse is pretty tired."

"Come outside, and I'll point the way," said Worley, stepping to the front door. "Zigzag down the mountain from here. Cut directly across the valley and go up that low butte in the distance. Ride along the crest until you see the highway which runs parallel to it for a short distance, then turns northwest. That's where you turn directly west. Is that clear?"

"Yes, it is, and thank you again," Bob said. "Come on, Linda."

They walked their horses to the lodge, found a faucet in the back and an old wooden tub in which they put water for the thirsty animals.

While their mounts rested, Linda and Bob settled under a sycamore, and Linda laid out the lunch. As Bob picked up a sandwich, he remarked, "I can't figure out those men."

"They struck me as rather odd," Linda said. "And they weren't telling the truth about the hoofprints. *Several* horses have been here."

"I see what you mean. The horse thieves could have brought stolen animals through this spot— even Prince Brownlee. The question is, where did they take them? The trail seems to end here."

Linda and Bob could find no answer and felt it was unwise to ask Worley and Garrant any further questions. They finished the lunch and Bob insisted they go at once.

"I have a feeling it isn't safe for just the two of us here. We'll come back next time with Bronco and Charlie."

His sister agreed but was reluctant to leave the mystery of Poe and the horse tracks unsolved. As she went to get Chica d'Oro, Linda was relieved to find that the palomino was as sprightly as ever after her brief rest.

With Bob in the lead, they rode down the mountain, crossed the valley, and went up on the butte which stretched out in a long, silty elevation. The going was precarious and the horses kept losing their footing on the loose earth. After a while, the two riders sighted the highway in the distance.

"It isn't so near as that fellow indicated," Bob said in disgust. "And it doesn't run parallel to this ridge."

"But we are headed out all right, aren't we?" Linda asked anxiously.

"Oh, sure," Bob called back. "But I certainly would never come on this silty, dangerous butte again. Take it easy!"

Just then the edge of the ridge near Linda gave way. Chica d'Oro and her rider went sliding down the slope onto a flat of sand. There she floundered for a moment, then began to sink.

"Quicksand!" Linda screamed.

The Pony's Warning　　　7

Linda threw herself off the pony and grasped a limb of chaparral on the fringe of the treacherous spot. In a moment, she had pulled herself to safety.

At Linda's cry, Bob had looked back. Instantly he slid his horse down the slope, building a loop with his rope at the same time. He pulled up short at the edge of the quagmire, and flung the noose about Chica d'Oro's neck. Then he fashioned a wider loop, and hurled it about her body, tightening it under the rump. Quickly he fastened the end of the rope to the toughest scrub root at hand.

"Oh, thank you!" Linda said in relief.

"I don't know how long this will hold," Bob said tensely. "Linda, ride Rocket to the highway for help," he ordered.

Linda mounted hastily, and galloped off. She reached the highway and waited anxiously. Tourists were the first to come along in a car. Frantically she waved for the driver to stop. But misunderstanding her gesture, the man waved back and continued on his way.

Tears sprang to Linda's eyes. The next car was a convertible holding a couple of grinning teen-age boys. It screeched to a stop.

"Hi, Annie Oakley!" one sang out.

Irked by their flippancy, Linda said shortly, "We have a horse down in quicksand over there. Please get someone to bring boards and help us."

"Sure, beautiful, at your service," the driver said and sped away. Linda's heart sank. The boys probably had no intention of finding help.

Linda tried not to picture the rope around Chica d'Oro fraying strand by strand, and the beautiful palomino sinking out of sight. She felt sick and grasped the saddle horn until her knuckles were white.

Suddenly at high speed came a jeep from which protruded several wide boards. The car was marked BENTLEY'S GARAGE, RUDDVILLE. The driver stopped and called out, "I'm Bentley. You the girl those boys said had a horse in quicksand?"

"Oh, bless them!" cried Linda, sorry she had mistrusted the boys. "This way!"

She turned at a gallop to lead him. With the jeep bumping along behind her, Linda pounded ahead, hoping against hope that she would not be too late. When she caught sight of Chica d'Oro, her heart leaped in relief. The filly seemed to have sunk but a fraction more in the quicksand.

"Good work, Linda!" Bob praised her.

The man in the jeep knew exactly what to do. Together he and Bob shoved boards under the pony's belly and laid them on each side of her to ride on should she topple over. Then Mr. Bentley fastened ropes to a piece of tarp he had brought along.

He gingerly stepped out on the boards and secured the tarp as a sling around the palomino's rump. Next he fastened each rope end to the back of the jeep, got behind the wheel, and inched ahead.

Chica d'Oro started thrashing up with her front hooves, and finally landed them on the firm fringe outside the quagmire. In a few minutes, she was standing beside Rocket, shaking herself and wearing a baffled expression.

Linda hugged her close. "I didn't put you in that place on purpose, baby," she explained. If the pony had had any such thoughts, she had already forgiven Linda, for she began to nuzzle the girl affectionately.

Mr. Bentley said, "We must post this quicksand. Kids hunting rabbits could get into it." He wrote QUICKSAND with his black crayon pencil on one of the boards and erected it on the bank.

"Ought to have a bright red rag on this so's it would attract attention," he murmured.

"Here," Linda said, and snatched off her red bandanna.

Mr. Bentley fastened it on top of the board. Bob

then attempted to thrust four one-dollar bills, the whole amount he carried in his pockets, into the hand of the jeep driver.

"Naw," protested the garage man, "I wouldn't take money for saving a horse's life. Drop into my place some day when you're in town and say hello. It's on the edge of Ruddville."

"We'll do that. Thanks again," Bob replied.

"You'll never know how much this means to me," Linda said warmly, brushing the sandy muck off Chica d'Oro.

"Just glad I got here in time," Mr. Bentley answered, and climbed into his jeep.

After he had driven off, Linda and Bob mounted and set off parallel to the highway. They rode in silence for a while. Both the Craigs were thoughtful and Linda was pale. At last she asked, "Do you think those men Worley and Garrant sent us out on that trail deliberately to—well, to get rid of us?"

Bob's face muscles tightened. "They were so familiar with the trail, they must have known about that bad spot."

It was late afternoon when Linda and her brother arrived at Indian Charlie's. Bronco and Charlie had returned and were inside the cabin. They listened attentively to the story of the mineral water company and the quagmire.

The two men looked serious. "Mineral Springs Bottling Company changed hands last fall," Charlie informed the others. "The old owner ran the hotel and water company. Many people went for cures." The Indian shook his head woefully. "The new owners are unfriendly. Closed the hotel, and do not want anybody around. Why do they not want to make money from the hotel?"

"That does seem odd," Bronco commented.

Linda nodded. "I want to go back there with you. But right now, Bronco, will you come out with me while I put the pony in her stall?"

"Sure, honey," he replied. As soon as they were outside he asked, "Well, what's on your mind?"

"Chica d'Oro," Linda replied. "I just *must* have her for my very own. How do you think I could get Charlie to sell her to me?"

"You might try asking him," Bronco said with a grin. "If he isn't interested in a cash sale, dangle a horse trade. There are a couple of fine young quarter horses down on Old Sol that may prove hard for him to refuse."

"Oh, thank you, Bronco, thank you," Linda said softly and hugged him.

By the time she had put Chica d'Oro into her stall, it was sundown. Linda prepared supper, then addressed Charlie.

"I thought I'd get Chica used to the saddle, if you don't mind."

"You do that," he replied.

"Charlie," she continued earnestly, "I'd like to own Chica. Will you sell her to me?"

The Indian gave the girl a long, stoic look. He said, "Never thought to sell young'un."

Linda swallowed. "Bronco says I may offer a couple of fine young quarter horses in trade for her. Would you like those, Charlie?"

A flicker of interest shimmered in the Indian's eyes. "Um-m, quarter horses. I will think about it."

After that, he would say no more. During supper, the group discussed the stolen Prince Brownlee, Luke Poe, and the men at the bottling company.

"I'm positive," Linda said, "that Fossil Mountain holds the answer to those mysteries. And maybe the secret of the lights. Shouldn't we go on a thorough search there?"

"We'd have to make it overnight," Bronco replied. "But your idea is a good one. If Luke Poe is a horse thief and he's hiding out near the mineral springs, maybe we can catch him in that vicinity."

While Bronco planned the trip in detail, Linda arose to get the men more coffee. Suddenly she gasped and pointed out the open window, whispering, "I saw a man's shadow!"

They all rushed into the moonlit yard. A man jumped up from a crouched position near the shed barn, flung himself onto a horse, and galloped away. The group realized it was useless to follow. By the time they could saddle up, he would have outdistanced his pursuers.

"I wonder if that was Luke Poe again," said Linda.

"Whoever the man was, I'll bet he was eavesdropping and heard our plans to go scouting on the mountain," Bob said.

"And you mean he may plan to ambush us!" Linda said worriedly as they reentered the cabin.

"We'll certainly have to be on the alert," Bronco remarked grimly. "Everybody up early and get your horses ready."

Linda looked at Charlie. Should she or should she not approach him on the subject of Chica d'Oro? Finally, taking a deep breath, she said, "Charlie, have you decided whether you are going to trade me young'un for the two quarter horses?"

The Indian did not answer at once and looked at the girl noncommittally.

Worry shadowed Linda's face. "I'm afraid something dreadful will happen to her when we're not here any more and you have to be away on the pipeline."

Charlie's black eyes regarded Linda steadily. Then he said slowly, "I have two grandsons living on a small ranch in the next valley. They are getting to be big boys. Should have horses."

Linda held her breath. A slight smile creased the Indian's face.

"I will trade."

"Charlie, oh, Charlie," Linda cried, "How wonderful of you!" She shook his hand vigorously. Then she did a spin in the middle of the floor and ended by hugging Bronco so suddenly and hard that he grunted.

"As soon as we return to Old Sol," Linda said in earnest enthusiasm, "I'm going to start trying to establish Chica's bloodline so I may obtain registration papers on her."

"How will you do that?" Charlie asked.

"Through the registration book of the Arabian Horse Association," Linda told him. "I'll check on each entry. Maybe I can find the owner of Chica d'Oro's dam."

"Which will take just about from now till you're an old lady," Bob said skeptically.

"Go to it, honey," Bronco encouraged her. "You may be lucky right off."

"I will. I just know I will," proclaimed Linda. "I feel it."

She went to bed too happy and excited to sleep. Chica d'Oro was hers! For hours the girl lay listening to the rain drum on the aluminum roof, but at last her eyes closed. When she opened them again it was Sunday morning and the sky was clear.

As soon as Linda could dress she ran out to the barn. Hugging her new possession, she told the pony softly, "You're mine, mine, all mine!" Then she added with a laugh, "Well, almost!" The filly nickered and nuzzled the girl's neck.

Linda gave the palomino a small can of oats, then laid a thick pad, an Indian blanket, and a saddle on her back. Chica d'Oro only turned her head curiously, touched the stirrup with her nose, and finished the oats.

Her new mistress cinched up the saddle and led the horse outside. She mounted and rode Chica d'Oro about the corral. The filly seemed to feel as good as Linda did. She tossed her mane and picked her dainty feet up high.

When Linda returned her to the barn, she found Bob, Bronco, and Charlie feeding the other horses. Linda unsaddled the pony and gave her a flake of hay, as Bronco strolled over to the stall.

"Get along all right?" he asked.

"She's the most wonderful horse in the world," Linda said firmly, her eyes shining. Grandfather Mallory smiled and patted the girl's arm.

In a short time, Bob, Linda, and Bronco were on their way. They took only one packhorse to carry the bedrolls, leaving the other behind as company for Gypsy. Along with canteens, the riders carried some of the food and a few accessories in tight packs on their saddles.

Linda noticed that Bronco was not taking the most direct route to Fossil Mountain. She asked why.

Bronco gave her a broad smile. "Since we can't get to our own church today, I'm going to take you and Bob to Cowboy's Church. It's on the outskirts of Ruddville."

"Cowboy's Church?" Linda repeated, puzzled.

"The preacher holds morning services outdoors," Bronco explained. "Riders come from all around and sit on their horses during the service. The horses stand as quiet as mice. After the service the ladies sell lunches to help pay off the mortgage on the church building."

"I'd like to go," said Linda.

"Me, too," Bob added.

The Ruddville Community Church yard was pleasantly shaded with blooming acacias under which were a few picnic tables. There were thirty horseback riders present, and as many people seated on folding chairs.

The minister officiated from a truck bed which also held the choir and a piano. He was a zealous young man with a commanding delivery and sense of humor, and preached an excellent sermon.

Mr. Bentley, who had helped rescue Chica d'Oro, assisted with the collection, and nodded, pleased, when Bob dropped into the plate the four one-dollar bills the garageman had refused at the quicksand pit.

Afterward Linda, Bob, and Bronco bought sandwiches, slaw, cherry pie, and milk from the church ladies, and enjoyed eating with the friendly congregation.

By early afternoon they were on their way again, approaching Fossil Mountain from a different direction to the one Linda and Bob had taken before. Near the foot of it, Bronco called a halt, took his rifle from the bedroll pack, and slipped it into his saddle boot.

"You must expect trouble," Bob remarked.

"One never knows," Grandfather Mallory replied. "I'd rather be safe than sorry."

They rode on again and came to a canyon of huge boulders and steep granite walls with fissures and rimrock caves.

Near the entrance, Linda stopped. Before her was a magnificent, creamy-white, single yucca, growing against a big, pinkish-red granite rock. She gazed at the tree-like plant in admiration. Oh, how I'd love to paint that! she thought.

Suddenly Chica d'Oro endeavored to back away, whickering uneasily. She pranced up and down, tossing her head. Linda looked sharply about the ground for a snake, but saw none.

Bob and Bronco rode up, and her brother asked, "What's eating Chica?"

"I don't know," Linda replied, troubled.

The two men circled, looking about. "There doesn't seem to be even a rabbit track around here," Bronco said. "Sometimes a strange scent from far away will cause a horse to gallivant a bit."

The rancher rubbed his chin as he looked at the big rock. Then he cast his eyes up the canyon. "There's a narrow cut ahead to the left. Beyond is a trail up the mountain. Let's move!"

As they rode into the ravine, single file, the palomino settled down to her easy gait. "Chica's all right now," Linda announced. "I think she was trying to tell us about something or someone behind that red rock."

"I think so, too," Bronco admitted. "But I didn't want to scare you by saying so."

"Why not?" Bob asked indignantly. "We could have caught the fellow."

"The fellow?" Bronco smiled wryly. "Half a dozen scoundrels could have been hiding in back of those rocks. We're not taking chances on being outnumbered."

"I didn't think of that," Bob admitted. "But we'd better keep a sharp eye out in case we're followed."

As they rode through the cut, the three riders stopped often to look back and listen for sounds of a person following them. But they saw no one. At last they came out of the ravine at a steep trail. It was some distance from the place where the mysterious lights had been seen. The riders climbed up and up.

"The lodge and Mineral Springs Bottling Company are around this curve to the right," Linda said finally. "But the frame building is so close to the mountainside you don't see it until you are right on it."

"Good!" Bronco exclaimed. "If Worley and Garrant are there maybe they won't see us either. We'll stay on this side of the cave and make camp in a secluded spot."

"Let's keep our eyes open for any clue to the horse thieves," Linda suggested, as the little group turned left. But they did not spot anything.

After they had climbed a little higher, they came to a creek. Bronco beckoned for them to cross it to a place on the far side enclosed by thick, bushy laurel and trees.

"This creek must be the same one we forded before," Linda said to Bob.

"It's the overflow from the dam above here," Bronco said, adding, "We can see the bottling company from this spot but no one can see us."

Although it was only five o'clock, the shadows were deep around the campers. In the growing dusk, they took care of their horses and fastened each to a bush with rope long enough so that they could move about. Contentedly the animals began to crop their supper of grass, seasoned with tufts of sage.

Bronco made a low fire of bark chips that soon became hot, but gave off very little smoke. Bob opened three cans of spaghetti and meatballs, and put them against the heat. Linda opened a can of green beans which they ate cold. There also were brown-bread sandwiches and apples.

Afterward Bronco said, "How about crawling in now and getting up at daylight for some early-bird detective work?"

"Let's," Linda agreed. "I'm tired." She checked Chica d'Oro, pulled off her boots, and snuggled down inside her sleeping bag.

Linda was awakened by her pony nuzzling the

side of her face and nickering plaintively. "How did you get loose?" she asked a bit crossly. "This is no time to play." With a sigh, she felt in the dark for her boots.

Chica d'Oro gave the girl a hard shove with her nose, whickering in terror. Then with frenzied screams, she took off up the side of the mountain.

"Bronco! Bob!" Linda cried as she heard a loud roar.

The two men awakened. They jumped up and began pulling on their boots.

"Run up the mountainside, Linda!" Bronco ordered. "The dam's given way!"

The other horses were threshing at their tethers, and whinnying in terror. While Bronco and Bob released them, Linda scrambled up the slope to Chica d'Oro. With the roar coming closer, the two men led the bolting, struggling horses up the silty slope. Bronco kept tight hold of Colonel's tie rope, knowing the other horses would follow him. By grabbing at scrub growth, he and Bob hauled themselves up the treacherous hill.

In a few seconds, Linda saw a high wall of water come crashing down through their camp with a deafening roar. The horses screamed in fright at the onrushing tumult.

Suspicious Cans 8

The flood boomed past the feet of Linda and her companions, wetting them with its spray, but leaving them safe.

How long can this last? the girl thought as the minutes dragged into hours.

Badly shaken, the group clung to their precarious footing for the rest of the night. As dawn broke, Linda, Bob, and Bronco looked down on a desolate scene. They shuddered at the devastation and shivered in their damp clothes.

Their camp spot was a shambles of mud, debris, and broken branches. The sleeping bags, cooking equipment, saddles, blankets, and bridles had been swept away.

"Oh!" Linda gasped. "Everything's gone!"

"Well, we're not!" Bob exclaimed cheerfully. "Thanks to that yaller young'un of yours."

"Come on, let's get down," Bronco urged, and began a sliding descent.

Linda and Bob followed, while the horses tagged along with Colonel. The Craigs picked up the ends of their horses' tie ropes to keep them from dragging through the mud.

Holding up one of them, Linda exclaimed, "Look, Bronco! Chica d'Oro chewed through the rope to get loose!"

"She must have felt the vibration of the dam giving way and sensed the danger, even before she heard the roar," Bronco said. "You have an intelligent, finely bred piece of horseflesh there, Linda."

Bob grinned. "For my money, she's the queen bee from now on."

In spite of their predicament, Linda gave him a warm smile. But in a moment she looked troubled again. "What do you think caused the dam to break, Bronco?" she asked. "Was it getting weak?"

"That was a well-built dam," he answered flatly. "Dynamite broke it."

"Dynamite?" Bob cried out.

"Yes."

"But who," Linda said, appalled, "would blow it up? And why?"

"Somebody who wants to get rid of us," Bob answered. He had been looking toward the Mineral Springs Bottling Company, untouched by the flood. "Maybe Worley or Garrant. After all, they ordered us off the place the first time we came here."

"And they sent us home by the quicksand route," Linda reminded the others.

"I wonder what their game is," Bronco mused. "Something big and illegal, I'd say, the way they're trying to keep it secret."

"Do you suppose *they're* responsible for the strange lights?" Linda surmised.

"Possibly," her grandfather agreed. "If those men are up to something crooked, they might be using the lights as a signal."

"Since Bob and I have seen both men and can identify them," Linda continued, "maybe that's why they want to get rid of us." She glanced about uneasily. "Do you think they know we weren't drowned?"

Bronco's forehead puckered. "Perhaps," he said. "One of them—or a henchman—must have followed us through the ravine yesterday and known we were camping here. The same spy might be watching in this direction now for signs of life."

"But why don't they just shoot us if they want us out of the way?" Bob asked abruptly.

"They want it to look like an accident," Bronco replied, "so the deaths can't be traced to them. Come on!" he ordered. "Let's go!"

Linda begged him to wait. "We came here to check on the bottling company," she said, "Please let's do a little sleuthing before we leave."

"What kind of sleuthing?" Bronco demanded.

"Will you stay with the horses while Bob and I tiptoe up and around the lodge and the office to find out what we can?" Linda proposed. "Yes, we'll be mighty careful," she answered the question she knew was coming.

Grandfather Mallory closed his eyes a few seconds as he mulled over the request. Finally he gave his consent. "Bob, whistle like a song sparrow if you need help and I'll come running."

Linda and Bob hurried forward, darting among the trees to escape detection. There was no evidence that anyone was around.

Just then Linda's attention was attracted to a heap of rubbish, evidently the dumping ground for the bottling company. Her eyes noted an empty gallon can of black dye.

Funny, she thought.

"What would they use black dye for at this place?" she asked Bob, who strode over to the pile. In it were several other empty cans of brown or black dye. "Worley and Garrant must be in the secret business of dyeing wigs!" he quipped.

Linda did not take time to laugh at her brother's remark. She said excitedly, "Bob, do you think they are in the secret business of dyeing horses?"

"You mean stolen horses?"

"Yes. Horse thieves change an animal's appearance and then sell it," Linda replied. "Why, Bob, if that's what happened to Prince Brownlee, we may never find him!"

She and her brother looked for more signs of the suspected nefarious business. They found two more cans, but nothing else.

"Let's take some of this evidence along," Linda proposed.

"Okay," Bob agreed, "but you know this may be only a wild guess."

"Let's call it a hunch," Linda countered as they each picked up a can.

The grounds yielded no further clues, and no one appeared from either building. Linda and Bob returned to Bronco, who was very interested in his granddaughter's theory.

"Are the horses brought to the bottling company for a dye bath," he speculated, "then taken away?"

"There's no place here to stable a horse," Linda spoke up. "Of course there *could* be a hideaway." But none was in evidence.

The puzzled trio decided to set off. Before leaving, Bob whipped out a jackknife and cut his horse's tie rope in two for a pair of reins. After unraveling a couple of ends, he fastened them to each side of Rocket's halter. Then he did the same for Chica d'Oro. He and Linda swung onto the horses' backs. Bronco, also riding bareback, led off, guiding Colonel in Indian style with his knees.

The bedraggled riders plodded their way carefully down the slope—a good distance from the creek. Reaching the bottom, they kept close to the foot of the mountain through an arid sandy area, and finally crossed the valley and headed for Charlie's cabin.

When they arrived, the Indian was not at home.

Hastily the visitors rubbed the hungry horses down, grained them, and tossed some hay into the feeding troughs.

Linda lingered in the barn for a few moments beside her pony. Gently she stroked the mane of the filly, who looked up from her food.

"Thank you," Linda said earnestly. "You saved our lives."

She now hurried from the barn and followed Bob and Bronco into the cabin. After they had changed into fresh clothes and washed up, Linda put on the coffee pot and made a quick breakfast of creamed chipped beef on toast.

While they were eating she asked, "What is the next step to find the missing Prince Brownlee?"

"I have a suggestion," said Bob. "Suppose I take those empty dye cans into Ruddville—even if I have to ride bareback. I'll find out, if possible, where they were purchased and by whom. That might help us locate the horse thief."

"A splendid idea," Bronco agreed. "And while you're in town buy us each a saddle, bridle, and horse blankets. You can arrange to have Linda's and mine sent out in the morning, when Charlie picks up supplies in his jeep." He signed a blank check and passed it over to Bob.

"What are you and Linda going to do?" Bob asked.

Linda smiled. "I'm going to teach Chica d'Oro some tricks."

"Well, good luck," Bob remarked.

Linda put several pieces of bread in her pocket and went to the corral. The pony greeted her with joyous nickering and a tossing of her mane.

"Would you like to do a few tricks, baby?" Linda asked her. She flipped out her handkerchief, and then stuffed it back into her shirt pocket with the corner sticking out.

Chica d'Oro immediately snatched it and waved the handkerchief up and down, proving that she did not forget her lessons. Then she received the first bread tidbit.

"Very good," Linda praised her. "Now let's see how smart you are at learning to nod yes."

She put the palomino through the same process as she had Speedy, the cutting horse. After half a dozen tries, Chica d'Oro responded perfectly to the cue. When Linda moved her cupped hand toward the filly's nose, the animal nodded her head up and down.

"Wonderful!" Linda said excitedly. "But you can't always be a yes horse. How about learning to say no?"

She tickled the inside of the pony's ear with the end of her finger to simulate a crawling bug. Chica d'Oro vigorously shook her head back and forth to get rid of the annoyance. After only a few tries she recognized the movement of Linda's finger toward her ear and shook her head automatically.

"That's great!" Linda said, feeding the filly her

expected treat. "How about giving me a good old horse laugh?"

Chica d'Oro looked at her young mistress expectantly with shining eyes. Linda took a bobby pin from her hair and gently pricked the horse on the bottom part of her upper lip. The pony raised her head, curled back her lip, and stuck out her lower one. Linda repeated the training until the horse "laughed" when the girl merely pointed her finger toward Chica's mouth.

"That's enough for today, sweetie," Linda said, and fed the palomino the remaining tidbits of bread. "Next time I'll teach you how to bow, to sit, to lie down and pull a blanket over yourself, and to pose like the 'End of the Trail' statue. Then we'll have a show, take up a collection, and buy a silver concha!"

Chica d'Oro whinnied. "Oh, you doll!" Linda exclaimed, unmindfully pointing a finger toward her pet. The horse rolled back her lip in a laugh!

As Linda walked toward the cabin, she met Bronco coming out. Both heard a whirring noise in the sky and looked up.

"A whirlybird!" Linda remarked. "I wonder where it's going."

She and Grandfather Mallory watched as the helicopter came closer. To their amazement, it began to settle down on a level spot near Indian Charlie's cabin.

"Who can it be?" Linda asked. "Someone from the pipeline company to see Charlie?"

Bronco did not reply. As Linda looked at him, she noticed that his jaw was set and his brow furrowed. This means he's worried, she felt.

Suddenly Linda thought, Could the 'copter contain men who have come to harm us? The same people who have tried it before?

California Windstorm 9

As Linda and Bronco waited tensely, the helicopter set down. The blades ceased to spin and the side door opened. Framed in it stood John Davis.

"Hello there!" he called.

Grins of relief spread over the faces of Linda and her grandfather, who cried, "Good to see you, Johnny! What brings you here?"

"I'm doing a little hedgehopping with this bird," Mr. Davis answered. "Went to Old Sol and heard you were here. Well, Linda, I have a surprise for you." He jumped down, then reached up a hand to assist a passenger.

"Doña!" exclaimed Linda, and as soon as the woman's feet touched the ground her granddaughter threw both arms around her.

Before she could say more, John Davis was lending a hand to a second passenger. Again Linda cried out in amazement. "Kathy! This is just marvelous!"

Kathy Hamilton, with honey blond hair and an apricot-tinted complexion, was sixteen and full of fun. She and Linda had known each other since childhood and recently Kathy had been a great solace to Linda.

"This is the grandest surprise ever," Linda said, hugging her attractive friend.

John Davis explained that he could stay only a short time. Mrs. Mallory would go back with him, but Kathy had permission to stay if there was room in the cabin.

"She wants to help solve the mysteries—unless they've already been solved," he explained.

Linda shook her head. "We haven't found Prince Brownlee, but we have a possible clue. Bob has gone to town to check on it."

"And the lights?" John Davis asked.

Bronco said, "We have a theory they're being used for some illegal purpose. But none of us has been able to find out what or by whom."

"I just thought of something," said Linda. "Do you suppose the lights are removed when they're not in use? That's why we can't find them?"

Bronco slapped his thigh. "I believe you have a point there, Linda."

Doña Mallory had started for the cabin. Linda ran after her, apologizing for her lack of hospitality. "May I get you some hot chocolate?" she asked.

"Yes, dear."

The whole group had cookies with the hot

chocolate while the Craigs' experiences were related. Mrs. Mallory sighed, then said to Kathy, "Are you sure you want to stay here?"

"I'd love the adventure," Kathy replied. "And I promise not to take any crazy chances."

Mrs. Mallory smiled. "I'll tell your mother that."

"Come see my wonderful surprise," Linda begged and led the visitors to the corral. "Look! Isn't that a beautiful palomino? She's mine! My very own!"

Linda's grandmother smiled. "She's a fine-looking pony. Tell me about her."

Kathy and John Davis admired Chica d'Oro as Linda briefed them all.

"Oh, I'm so happy for you," Kathy said enthusiastically.

Mr. Davis added his praise, then said he must leave. Kathy's extra clothes and blankets were brought from the helicopter, and a few minutes later the pilot and Grandmother Mallory took off.

"Would you like to go for a ride—bareback?" Linda asked Kathy.

"Bareback? Well—"

"That won't be necessary," Bronco spoke up. "I came across an old saddle of Charlie's. It will fit Gypsy." He led the way to the barn and showed the well-worn black leather saddle to Kathy. "Could you manage with this?"

"Oh, yes, and I'd love to go. Maybe we can do some detective work, Linda!"

Her friend grinned. "I'll take you to the spot where there's the most beautiful yucca I've ever seen." As Kathy looked puzzled, Linda went on. "Near it is a huge rock. Chica d'Oro shied away from it the other day. Maybe somebody was hiding—and left a clue."

Bronco looked intently at the girls. "Don't forget your promise to Doña. In fact, I think I'd better come along." ·

"Please do," Linda said. "I'll fix some lunch to take with us."

Grandfather Mallory rode Colonel bareback with no halter, while Linda put the hackamore on Chica d'Oro. The three riders set off, with Linda leading the way. By taking a shortcut, they arrived at the beautiful yucca in less time than the day before.

As they approached the entrance to the gorge, a sudden sharp explosion echoed within its rocky walls. The riders reined up.

"That sounded like a shot!" Linda exclaimed. Seeing Kathy's uneasy expression, she added, "But it might have only been someone hunting game."

"Just the same," Bronco said, "I'll ride up first and have a look. You two wait here."

The girls watched until he disappeared around a distant bend in the gorge. They walked their mounts over to the yucca in front of the red rock.

"Isn't it lovely?" Linda exclaimed.

She and her chum sat for a few minutes admiring the creamy color of the bloom. Then Linda's eyes fastened on the rock. She decided no one was hiding behind it because Chica d'Oro was not acting worried the way she had the day before.

Nevertheless, Linda looked again at the red rock, wishing that she could see through it. In a moment, curiosity began to exceed caution.

Linda said to Kathy, "Let's take a look back there."

The girls dismounted and slowly went toward the rock, scarcely breathing. When they reached the back of it, Linda and Kathy gave sighs of relief. No one was there, but Linda found a cranny just big enough for a horse to stand in, and there were horseshoe prints visible.

As she looked closer at them, Linda noted something else and picked it up. "A purple electric light bulb!" she cried.

"What a wonderful clue!" Kathy exclaimed.

Linda was elated. She said excitedly, "This must have been dropped by someone connected with those strange lights. They're probably strung on wires and laid down when needed."

"But where," asked Kathy, "would you get any current way out here?"

"Powerful batteries," Linda answered, "or even a generator. But don't ask me where *that* is. It may be stationary or the portable type carried on a truck."

Linda put the light bulb in her pocket, and the two companions fell silent, each trying to guess the meaning of the strange lights.

"I wonder what's taking Bronco so long," Kathy said uneasily.

"We ought to ride after him and find out," Linda replied, plainly tempted to do so.

"But he ordered us to stay here," Kathy said, "and he's the trail boss today."

"You're right," Linda conceded with a grin. "Let's get out the lunch. He ought to be back soon."

The girls unpacked the sandwiches and tomatoes. As they ate, Kathy remarked how still it was. "Even the horses aren't moving."

"Unusually still," Linda said. "The horses should be foraging the growth. I don't like it."

Suddenly alarmed, the girls became aware of a current of air against their faces. The yucca began to sway, and the dangling rope reins on Chica d'Oro's halter started to swing. A sound like agonized wailing came from around the rocks.

"We must find Bronco and get out of here!" Linda cried.

At that moment, the girls heard a faint shout in the gorge and saw Bronco galloping around the bend. "Ri-ide—home!" he called, waving his arms to them to go ahead. "A windstorm's coming!"

Kathy had no trouble mounting her horse, but Chica d'Oro proved to be a problem. The wind, sand, and eerie sound had spooked the pony. She sidled away and circled, tossing her head and whinnying, when Linda started to swing onto her back. Linda pivoted the pony fast twice, and in the following moments, while Chica d'Oro stood confused and quiet, the girl managed to mount her. She galloped after Kathy toward Charlie's cabin.

That was where Chica d'Oro now wanted to go, so Linda kept only one hand on the reins. With the other, she pulled her slipping kerchief over her face and held it there against the stinging, gritty dust.

Suddenly one of Chica d'Oro's hoofs went into a chuck hole and she crashed down on her knees. Linda was thrown violently over the pony's head. The breath was knocked out of the girl, and she lay stunned.

Linda was conscious, however. With her face down in her arms, she began gasping for breath. When the anxious girl opened her eyes a slit, she noted that her sleeves were torn. The wind, dust, and sand were a swirling fury by now. She could see nothing around her.

"Chica d'Oro!" Linda called weakly. "Baby!" But she could scarcely hear the sound of her own voice.

Linda pulled herself to her knees, but had to keep her head bowed against the stinging gale. She pulled her kerchief down to unmuffle her voice, and desperately called her pony again and again.

Finally she heard a plaintive whinny. Linda kept calling to direct the palomino to her, and in a few minutes there came the soft, blessed nuzzling against her neck. At the same moment, she heard Bronco's voice behind her.

"You all right?" he shouted over the storm as he dismounted.

"Y-yes. Just a spill."

Bronco helped the girl to her feet and she caught hold of Chica d'Oro's mane to steady herself. Linda pressed her face against the warm flesh of the pony's neck, grateful that she was not badly hurt and had stayed with her.

As Linda adjusted the kerchief over her face again, Kathy rode up. "Linda!" she cried. "Are you hurt?"

"I'll be all right," Linda insisted.

Bronco helped her mount. "Linda, go first!" he called over the wind. "Stick together!"

The girl gave Chica d'Oro a loose rein. The palomino started off as if she knew the way, but at a slow gait, limping badly. Linda was unhappy at having to add her weight to the little horse, but she dared not dismount in the raging windstorm. Frequently she reached out a hand to Chica d'Oro's neck, petting her gently, and felt an answering quiver of flesh.

Suddenly the filly slid down a nearly perpendicular embankment. Linda grasped hard at the handhold to keep from plunging over the horse's head. They landed in a wash, however, and the sides provided a little protection.

Bronco, who had followed with Kathy, said this was a longer way home, but a more sheltered one. After following the gully for a while, the riders emerged close to a trail leading to Charlie's cabin.

When they were almost there, Bob crossed their path, fighting his way back from town. At his dumbfounded look, Kathy's eyes sparkled sideways at him across the top of her kerchief. "Hi!" she called. "I came to join your detective force."

"Great!" said Bob.

Further conversation was impossible until the riders reached Charlie's barn. Then there was a quick exchange of stories. Bob said a Ruddville hardware man had told him the cans of dye were not sold in Ruddville, but probably had been purchased in Los Angeles.

"There was no identifying mark to any store," Bob went on, "so I guess it would be impossible to trace the cans to a particular place. When I suggested to the hardware man that the dye might have been used on horses, he remarked, 'It wouldn't be the first time horse thieves have used that method of disguise in their underhanded business.'"

"Then we might be on the right track!" Linda exclaimed. "If so, I only hope Prince Brownlee hasn't been shipped so far away we can't find him."

"If he has been dyed a different color," Kathy interposed, "how could you recognize him even if you saw him?"

"I'm sure I could," Linda said. "Every horse has certain characteristics, just like a person. No dye is going to change that. Prince Brownlee was a high stepper. He held his head erect and his gait was in perfect rhythm. When I went up to him, he shook his head and snorted."

During this conversation, Bronco had brought out some of Charlie's horse liniment and was applying it to Chica d'Oro's leg. When he had finished, they all went into the cabin and the girls closeted themselves in the supply room.

"We'll have to sleep together without moving," Linda said with a grin, "or one of us will fall out of bed!"

Linda applied ointment to her own scraped skin. "Now I know exactly what a lemon must feel like on a grater," she said, laughing, and put on a fresh blouse.

A little later, when Charlie came home, the cabin was filled with the aroma of frying steaks. While Linda and Kathy set the table, they told him about their afternoon adventure and the light bulb Linda had found.

The Indian frowned. "I do not like that. Those men are too close."

He said he would examine every inch of ground as he walked the pipeline to see if he could pick up any suspicious tracks made by Luke Poe—or others.

When the group arose the next morning, they noted that both Charlie and the jeep were gone. He drove in just as they were finishing breakfast, and everyone hurried outside to help him unload the riding equipment and groceries he had brought. When Bronco reached the car, Charlie handed him a telegram.

"It came to the Ruddville office just before dawn," he said.

Bronco opened the envelope as Linda, Bob, and Kathy watched in silent concern.

Mr. Mallory scanned the message quickly and scowled. "This is from Cactus Mac," he announced, and read aloud, "Bad trouble here. Return pronto."

Ranch Trouble 10

Bob and Linda exchanged worried looks.

"Trouble?" Bob said, taking the telegram from Bronco. "What kind of trouble? Why didn't Mac say what it was?"

Bronco smiled dryly. "You all know Mac. He'd rather tell you the whole story himself with all the dramatic details."

"But what do you suppose is the matter?" Linda asked anxiously. "And why didn't Cactus Mac use the two-way radio to tell us?"

"Probably he couldn't get us," Bronco answered.

"Or the telegram might not even be from Cactus Mac," Linda suggested. "The Fossil Mountain men could have sent it. Perhaps we're too close to finding out what they're up to—especially if they're tied in with the horse stealing."

Bronco rubbed his chin and squinted his eyes in speculation. "Maybe, maybe not. But if it is a scheme to pull us off the scent," he said firmly, "we're not going to fall for it!"

He strode into the cabin and turned on the shortwave set. He could get no reply from Old Sol.

"Either these batteries are gone or else those in the ranch set." He turned searching eyes on Linda and Bob. "I believe you had better start for home at once and take Kathy with you. Find out if anything did happen, or whether this message was a hoax."

"And what about you?" Bob asked.

"I'll stay here as guard," Grandfather Mallory replied, "in case something peculiar takes place in this area."

"How will I get a message to you? By telegram?" Bob questioned.

"Good idea. Wire me tomorrow. Charlie or I will ride into Ruddville and pick it up."

All this time Linda had been silent. She was worried about Chica d'Oro. Finally she said, "But Bronco, I can't go today. My pony is too lame to ride and I'd be afraid to leave her. Something might happen to her when you and Charlie are away."

"Don't you worry about Chica d'Oro, honey," Bronco said. "I'll take good care of her. It'll be good for her sprained leg to give it some easy exercise— keep it from getting stiff—so I'll take her with me if I go out of sight of the cabin."

"Well, all right then," Linda agreed. "When shall we leave?"

"Better start as soon as possible," Bronco replied. "Ride one of the packhorses and take the other one along. You have no sleeping bags or cooking equipment, but you can ask one of the ranchers to put you up for the night." He took out his billfold and passed several tens over to Bob.

"I'll pack my things and fix a lunch for us to take," Kathy offered.

When Rocket, Gypsy, and the other two horses were ready for the journey, with packets of food and canteens filled, Linda turned to Chica d'Oro. Despite a limp, the filly had been dancing around Linda, expecting to go along. Now the girl led her into the stall and hugged her close.

"I'll be back soon for you," she told the pony, "or else you'll be coming to me."

As Linda rode off, Chica d'Oro whinnied jealously, kicked at the door, and limped back and forth behind it. Poor baby! her owner thought.

Bob had noted landmarks on the ride up to Charlie's: an exceptionally large, twisted Joshua tree, an abandoned mine shaft, a Mojave desert shack, and rock formations, so he had no trouble finding the route home. Nevertheless, he and Linda consulted their new compasses frequently.

In the evening, they stopped at a ranch to ask for lodging, and the pleasant owner was glad to have them. There was a fenced-in shed yard for the horses. On the big screened porch in the back, along with laundry tubs and an ironing board, two cots were set out for Linda and Kathy. Bob would sleep on hay in the barn.

After the riders had joined the family for a hot, boiled ham dinner, they went to bed early and slept soundly. At dawn, they were in the saddle again.

It was forenoon when they drew near to Old Sol. Linda said huskily, "I sort of have the whim-whams coming back here now. I wonder what we'll find."

"We'll know soon enough," Bob replied grimly.

In a few moments, Linda, Bob, and Kathy mounted a low rise and looked down into the shallow basin where the ranch house and main buildings lay in a cluster. For a second, they stared, astonished.

"The windmill's gone!" Linda exclaimed.

Together the three riders spurred down toward the corral. Bales of hay were lying around it, some of them broken open. As the Craigs dismounted beside a damaged water trough, Grandmother Mallory came hurrying from the ranch house to greet them. Cactus Mac emerged from the barn.

"Thank goodness you three are here!" Mrs. Mallory said. "Where's Bronco!" she inquired just as Cactus Mac joined them and asked the same question.

Bob explained. "Bronco thought that whoever made the trouble here might have done it to get us away from Charlie's place, so he stayed there to keep his eye on things."

"Those varmints must want to keep you away

from there pretty bad," Cactus Mac growled. "Just wait till you see the damage."

"We noticed that the windmill is down," Bob said.

"And the fences are cut. Come on, I'll show you," Mac offered.

Linda had been looking around. "Wait a minute!" she said. "Where's Rango? He's usually here to welcome us."

"He's gone," Cactus Mac blurted. "Disappeared the same time the damage was done, I guess."

"Oh, no!" Linda breathed in dismay.

"But how could anyone walk close enough to Rango to get hold of him?" Bob asked. "He always barked loudly when anyone came around."

Cactus Mac could not answer this. "They got him away somehow before he could sound an alarm," the foreman declared. "Maybe they gassed him and then shot one of those new tranquilizer drugs at him—the kind they give wild animals when they want to bring 'em back alive."

"And then they carried him off!" Linda wailed.

"If Rango is not dead, he'll try to come home," Mrs. Mallory assured the girl, patting her arm.

"How about our water supply?" Bob asked.

"Fortunately the tank was full," Cactus Mac replied, "and I've got an old jack pump workin'. It'll do till this windmill can be repaired and stood up again."

"Some of the vanes of the wheel are broken," Linda observed, frowning.

"Worse'n that," Cactus Mac said, "the varmints cut fences near the house. The cattle ready for shipment wandered out along the highway," he went on bitterly. "Three good steers were killed before we could round up all the strays."

The Craigs went with him to the fences. Bob noted that a hasty mending job had been done by twisting wires together. "We'll have to get new wire strung in these spots," he said.

"Yup," Cactus Mac agreed, "and a real tough job that is, too. We'd better start on it first thing in the morning."

"Was the sheriff notified of the damage?" Linda asked.

"Right away," Cactus Mac replied. "The sheriff and a deputy came out that same night and looked the place over. Later they picked up two suspects, but they weren't the ones."

"Did you find anything that someone might have dropped or did you see any tracks?" Bob asked.

"No footprints," Cactus Mac replied. "But over by the windmill were tread marks from the tires of a pickup truck. It was used to pull the windmill over. In the middle of the night, we heard the mill go down. I ran out as the truck was speeding off."

The conversation was interrupted by the sound of the metallic triangle being beaten to call the ranchers to lunch. The young people followed Mrs. Mallory to the house and went through the kitchen. Luisa stopped the Craigs. She held the two slender young people off at arm's length and exclaimed in her Mexican tongue. "*Delgado!* So skinny! You eat a lot of Luisa's pork pie. That put some fat on those stick-out bones."

"Don't you worry!" Bob declared with a grin, sniffing the delicious aroma. "We'll eat plenty. Just bring it on!"

Besides the steaming pie, Luisa served crisp green salad, corn bread, and apple dumplings for dessert. Kathy declared she had never enjoyed a meal more.

When they finished, Bob went at once to the two-way radio and tried to contact his grandfather. He failed, so sent a telegram.

A little later Kathy said she must go home and Bob offered to take her. He saddled one of the horses for her and brought it to the ranch house door.

"Let me know, Linda, what happens," Kathy said as she mounted.

"I will," her chum promised, and stood gazing after the couple as they trotted down the lane. Kathy's parents operated the Highway House, a restaurant and souvenir shop on the main road. They lived in a rambling, split-level dwelling alongside it.

When Kathy and Bob were out of sight, Linda

began a bit of sleuthing around the ranch house grounds to see if she could figure out anything about the mysterious saboteurs and in what direction Rango might have gone.

The question is, did they take him, or after he woke up, did he pick up their trail and follow them? she asked herself.

Linda got down on hands and knees to examine the ground thoroughly. There was a crisscrossed confusion of tire tracks, horseshoe prints, and boot marks. But finally the girl was able to make out the dog's toeprints.

Now where do they go? she wondered, following them slowly back and forth between the house, the corral, and the barn. She traced the marks to the rear of the stable. Here they ended.

That proves Rango was stolen. Linda's eyes blazed. I don't know who is worse—a horse thief or a dognapper!

Cactus Mac found her staring into space and asked what was on her mind. When he heard, the foreman said, "You got a good right to be hoppin' mad. Thar ain't any kind o' thief what ain't a sneakin' wretch." After a moment he added, "I'm goin' to jeep into Lockwood. Want to go along and clear that thar brain o' yours?"

Linda smiled. "Mac, you're an old darling. Yes, I'd love to go. I'll run in and tell Doña."

When they reached Lockwood, Cactus Mac said his errand would take half an hour. A sudden idea came to Linda, who said she would get out and meet him later in front of the deputy sheriff's headquarters.

She walked a couple of blocks, and entered the office. Linda introduced herself to Deputy Randall and asked him whether any trace had been found of the shepherd dog Rango.

"Not a thing yet, Miss Craig," he replied kindly. "But we have a broadcast out on him. We'll let you know just as soon as something comes in."

"Thank you," Linda said, unable to keep the disappointment out of her voice.

She explained to Deputy Randall that she, her brother, and grandfather were working on the theft of Prince Brownlee, and told about the cans of dye.

"Good detecting," the man commended her. "I'll get in touch with the sheriff up there and talk it over."

Linda spoke of the damage at the ranch and was dismayed to learn that the authorities had no clues yet to the identity of the perpetrators. "We're working on it, though," the deputy assured her.

Linda thanked him and left, wondering how long it would be before the enemy might strike again. She and Cactus Mac reached home in the late afternoon.

During dinner that evening, Linda said to Bob and Grandmother Mallory, "Don't you think we should stand watch tonight in case any men come to cause more damage?"

"Yes," Bob agreed. "I'll do it."

Grandmother Mallory shook her head. "Not all night," she said. "Cactus Mac can spell you."

Linda wanted to offer her services for part of the time but knew Doña would never permit this. It was arranged that Bob would be on duty until midnight, then Cactus Mac would relieve him.

That night Linda slept fitfully. She kept waking up to wonder what was happening outdoors. Finally, at eleven-thirty, a faint noise brought her to the window on a run. Linda listened intently.

Then, hurriedly, throwing on a robe and slippers, she slipped outdoors and along the back patio which ran the length of the house.

The noise came from the barn, she thought. It sounded like an animal, but it could be a trick by those marauders to ambush Bob and do more damage.

Staying in the shadows of the oak trees, she moved cautiously. Nothing was in sight. Linda ran around to the rear of the barn and came up the far side of it. At the front corner, she stopped. Flattening herself against the side wall, she peered around.

Where's Bob? she thought, worried, then looked straight ahead.

In the moonlight shining onto the barn door, stood Rango. Scarcely able to move, he came limping toward the girl with a couple of weak yelps.

Linda ran to him, sat down, and gathered the dog

into her lap. "Oh, poor fellow!" she exclaimed. "Poor Rango! You're hurt! Bob! Bob!" she called.

Almost instantly her brother appeared, racing across the yard. "Linda, what are you doing here? Well, I'll be—" He leaned down to pat the dog. "So you came home, old fellow."

Bob explained that he had been on his way back from a quick patrol of the fence when he heard Linda's cry.

"Rango has been injured," his sister said. "Let's carry him into the house."

Bob carefully shifted the big dog into his own arms and took him into the kitchen. Quickly Linda brought a pan of milk. As Rango stood, trembling, lapping it up, they watched him anxiously. "Look at those ugly marks on his legs," Linda said.

"He's been trussed up," Bob remarked angrily.

"How did he ever get loose?" Linda asked.

Bob shook his head, equally puzzled.

While Rango finished drinking, Linda quietly got an old blanket to make a pallet on the floor, and a pan of warm water and a sponge.

When the milk was gone, Bob stretched Rango out on the pad to wash his wounds. Deftly Linda took off the pet's collar.

"Bob!" she said a moment later, "I think there's a note wrapped around his collar!"

She removed the piece of tablet paper from the leather band. "It *is* a note, but oh, Bob, the message is dreadful!"

"What does it say?" Bob demanded.

Tears had sprung to Linda's eyes. "It says—it says, 'We have your palomino. If you want the horse back, get five hundred dollars for us and follow instructions!'"

Strange Orders 11

Linda and Bob sat back on their heels, too stunned to speak for a moment. Then Bob said, "They can't have Chica d'Oro. Bronco said he'd take good care of her. I believe this is just a trick to get money."

"Maybe," Linda said soberly, trying to make herself believe this. She read on: "Put fifty ten-dollar bills in outside mailbox by closed-up hamburger stand at junction of Ridgecrest and Vallejo roads at ten o'clock tomorrow morning. Palomino will be left at Silver Sage Ranch."

"I still think it's a trick," Bob declared confidently. "We should ignore this except to tell the sheriff."

Linda was not convinced. "Suppose Bronco was overpowered," she suggested ominously.

"Maybe. We'll have to find out," Bob replied with a taut face.

"Let's call Deputy Randall right away," Linda urged.

Bob agreed and hurried into the living room to

telephone. Meanwhile, Linda found a tube of ointment and gently applied some to the raw marks on Rango's legs.

When Bob returned, he said, "Deputy Randall talked with the sheriff in Charlie's county. He'll send one of his deputies out in a jeep to Charlie's right away, to see whether Bronco and he and Chica d'Oro are all right."

Linda looked up at the kitchen clock. "It's past midnight. It'll be morning before we hear anything."

At this moment, the kitchen door opened and Cactus Mac walked in. He was dumbfounded to hear the turn of events. "Guess I've lost my job as guard," he said.

"We're not sure the people who sent the note are the same as those who tried to wreck the ranch," Linda told him. "I think you'd better watch, and we'll let you know the minute we hear from the sheriff."

The foreman nodded and departed. As Linda and Bob went to their rooms, they were glad that Doña had not awakened. She was up at sunrise, however, to answer the ringing telephone. Her grandchildren flew to her side.

"Deputy Randall?" they heard her say. "Yes, Bob is here. I'll let you talk to him."

The conversation was short and ended with Bob's saying, "We'll be in Lockwood at eight."

After hanging up, he explained to the others,

"Bronco is all right. But three masked, armed riders surprised him and Charlie Tonka last night, and took Chica d'Oro at gunpoint." He paused, seeing Linda's stricken look.

Bob put his arm across her shoulders and went on, "We're to follow the instructions in the ransom note. First we're to go to Deputy Randall and give him the note. Then he'll accompany us to the bank in Ruddville. Bronco has arranged with the president to give us the money."

Mrs. Mallory stood up very straight and said, "I hope those lawbreakers will be caught soon and severely punished." But her voice trembled ever so slightly, indicating to Linda and Bob that she was worried about her husband's safety.

By eight o'clock, Linda and her brother were walking into the deputy's office. He greeted the Craigs affably. Bob took the pencil-scribbled ransom note from his pocket and handed it over.

"We'll have this checked for fingerprints," Randall said, giving it to a man at the desk. "And when we get the money, I'll have the bank make a record of the serial numbers, and keep a set here. By the way, your grandfather also said to tell you to have Cactus Mac load a couple of three-year-old quarter horses into the trailer. Take them with you to the Silver Sage Ranch and then bring the horses on to Charlie Tonka's place."

"And where is the Silver Sage Ranch?" Linda inquired.

"About fifty miles out on the Sierra Highway," the deputy informed her. "You can't miss it."

"Do you think the ranch folks are in cahoots with the horse thieves?" Linda asked him.

"No, I don't believe that," Randall replied. "I know them—people by the name of Larsen, and a real nice couple. Board horses and rent pasture. I think that they are just being used."

Deputy Randall went on. "We can start for the bank at once." He took his ten-gallon hat from its hook. "The sheriff is putting a man in the hamburger stand where you're to leave the money, and staking out a couple on the hills behind it."

"I'd like to call home before we go," Linda put in quickly, "and tell my grandmother to have everything ready."

"Go ahead."

"Use this phone," the man at the desk said.

Linda talked to Mrs. Mallory, who was relieved to know deputies would be hidden at the ransom spot, but alarmed about the task ahead of the young people. She warned them to be cautious and promised to give their message to Cactus Mac.

Linda and Bob went to the bank with Randall and took care of the money transaction with the president. Finally Linda and Bob returned to Old Sol. Cactus Mac had the two chestnut quarter horses loaded in a three-horse trailer hitched to the pickup.

"That third stall's for Chica d'Oro," he said hopefully.

"Oh, yes." Linda smiled, wishing she were as certain as she sounded.

Hurriedly she and Bob changed from town clothes into riding jeans. As they climbed into the truck beside Cactus Mac, Mrs. Mallory admonished them, "Just put the money in that mailbox, pick up the horse, and leave the catching of those bounders to the sheriff." Her grandchildren consented.

After a long drive down the sun-baked highway, Cactus Mac turned off on a dusty side road. He had no trouble finding the closed hamburger stand and mailbox at the junction of two little-used back-country dirt roads. The surrounding terrain was barren and rough.

Quietly Bob slipped the packet of money into the box. Then the three drove back toward the highway.

"There was supposed to have been a deputy in that shack, and two more hidden on the hills behind it," Linda remarked. "It gives me the creeps to think that we were being watched."

"Don't forget there was probably at least one of the horse thieves spying to make sure we left the money," Bob reminded her.

"Yup," added Cactus Mac, "and *he* was being watched by them thar deputies."

After they had swung into the main road, two

highway patrol cars passed them at intervals, going in opposite directions.

"I have an idea they too are on the lookout for your palomino," Bob said.

"How will the thieves get her to the Silver Sage without being seen?" Linda asked. Then a dreadful thought came to her. "Maybe they dyed Chica d'Oro! If the authorities are looking for a palomino, they might not recognize her!"

"If those hoss thieves did that," said Cactus Mac vehemently, "I'll tar an' feather 'em!"

An hour and a half later, when they drove up to the Silver Sage Ranch, Linda and her companions saw a group of neat buildings and white corral fences enclosing squares of pasture. Different sizes and types of horses were nibbling contentedly. In a riding ring, a dressage group of eight were practicing a formation drill with their gaited mounts.

As Cactus Mac brought the pickup to a stop, a tall, rawboned, sandy-haired woman in tan frontier pants and a cream shirt strode toward them with a pleasant smile.

Linda jumped out excitedly, saying, "Are you Mrs. Larsen?"

"Yes, I am," the woman replied. "What can I do for you?"

"I'm Linda Craig. We've come for the palomino that was left here for me."

"Well, a palomino was left here today," she said

kindly, "but not for you. It came in a rental trailer from the city for a Helen Andrews."

"Maybe they gave the wrong name," Bob suggested.

"Would you know the horse?" Mrs. Larsen asked.

"Oh, yes," Linda replied.

"Follow me then," the woman said, "and see if this is the one."

All of them went with her as she led the way to a box stall with a private paddock. Inside, stood a palomino mare with her ribs showing.

"She needs fattening up," Mrs. Larsen commented.

"That isn't Chica d'Oro," Linda said sadly. "My horse was stolen. We paid a ransom and she was to have been left here."

"Could our pony have been put somewhere around the place without your knowing it?" Bob asked.

"We'll just see about that," Mrs. Larsen said, and led the way to the big barn.

Chica d'Oro was not there. Nor was she in any of the two long rows of box stalls, the pastures, or the huge feed shed, packed to the rafters with hay.

"We've been duped, Linda," said Bob.

"I'm sorry, young lady," Mrs. Larsen told the girl, who was pale and silent. "But I'm certainly obliged to you for warning me of horse thieves on the loose. I'll post an extra guard."

Cactus Mac put in, "Thank you, ma'am, for your trouble. We'll be gettin' along."

Discouraged, the searchers drove back to the hamburger shack mailbox. The money was still in it. A deputy sheriff showed himself at the door of the boarded-up stand.

"My horse wasn't left at the ranch," Linda told him.

"Better take your money then," the deputy replied. "We'll stay on guard tonight and pick up anybody who comes around."

Cactus Mac buttoned the packet of money inside his shirt, and headed back to the highway. They stopped at a roadside restaurant for a belated lunch, but despite Bob's urging, Linda was not able to eat much.

"We'll follow this highway to a spot close to Charlie's," Mac told them as they climbed back into the truck. "Then you two can cut cross-country to his place on horseback."

Ahead of them the road wound around the foot of a high hill. Linda's eye caught something small and white waving on the hilltop. What can that be? she wondered, puzzled.

As they neared a sharp bend, Linda saw that the curve of the highway paralleled a deep ravine on their right. Seconds later a car zoomed around the bend in their lane!

Cactus Mac turned the truck out of the way so sharply to avoid a head-on collision that the horse trailer nearly rocked over. For a moment, it seemed to Linda that they would surely go off the highway into the chasm. She clapped her hand over her mouth to stifle a scream.

But Cactus Mac held the truck and the trailer to the road. He proceeded slowly around the curve and stopped. The foreman nervously mopped his perspiring face.

"Oh, Mac, you're a marvelous driver," said Linda. "We and the horses might have been killed!"

Bob agreed. "If it hadn't been for the way you handled the outfit, Cactus," he said soberly, "that crazy driver might have put us at the bottom of the ravine."

"Do you think," Linda asked, "that he might have done it deliberately? Just before we came to the bend I saw something white waving on top of the hill. It could have been a signal to that car to say we were coming."

"Maybe this whole horse-thieving setup was just a ruse to get us out here and pull off another 'accident,'" Bob said worriedly.

"That's right," growled Cactus Mac and pointed to a small dirt road which led out of a stand of trees onto the highway. "Varmints could've been waiting right thar."

Bob swung down from the truck and hurried to the rutted path, with Linda directly behind him. "Here are tire marks," he said triumphantly, "and they don't go any farther down this road. It looks as if a car only drove in and turned around."

Suddenly Linda said, "Look! Boot prints! One of the men got out. Bob, let's remember these left and right prints—size, shape, and— Oh! There's a star mark on the bottom."

Bob whipped a piece of string from his pocket and measured the length and width, tying knots to indicate the dimensions. He and Linda hurried back to the truck and requested Cactus Mac to report the whole incident to Deputy Randall, give him the string, and mention the star trademark.

"I'll do that," he agreed. "But if I can lay my hands on that thar road hog, I'll give 'im a lickin' on my own account!"

Cactus Mac drove on and at last pulled over to the side of the highway, where they unloaded the horses. Bob and Linda saddled them. As they waved and rode off toward Indian Charlie's, Cactus Mac headed the truck and trailer for Rancho del Sol.

When the two riders arrived at the cabin, Bronco and Charlie were waiting for them. "I'm glad you made it safely," said Grandfather Mallory. "But where's Chica d'Oro?"

He was told the story of the double cross. Then Linda asked, "The men who attacked you—did they leave any kind of clues, like boot prints?"

"Come to think of it, they did. But they looked like anybody else's—nothing special about them."

Linda said she would like to see them, just the

same. When she and Bob looked at the prints, Bob exclaimed, "They're just like the ones we saw. See the star mark!"

"Which could prove a lot *or* a little," Bronco remarked philosophically. "We'll tell the sheriff first chance we get. One of the things the horse thieves did was to take my two-way radio set."

"So that's why we couldn't get you," said Linda. "Any more trouble here?"

"No. I'm convinced the thieves are taking only blooded stock," Bronco decided. "For that reason, Charlie's horses are safe and we needn't stay here. I believe I'm needed at home. By the way, those mysterious lights haven't been turned on once since you left."

"Do you think that's because we're here?" Linda asked.

"Perhaps." Grandfather Mallory added, "I forgot to tell you something. When the deputy drove me back here from Ruddville, we picked up Charlie and followed Chica's tracks to Fossil Mountain, but lost them there."

"Sheriff is sending another jeep for the search tomorrow," Charlie put in.

Linda was excited at this information. "Please, Bronco, may Bob and I stay here and try to pick up their trail?"

"That's a great idea," Bob said. "On horseback we can get into some of those rocky spots on the mountain where even a sheriff's jeep can't go."

Bronco gave his consent but requested, "If you find something, leave a note here for the sheriff's men. They're going to check up on these premises each morning until the palomino is found."

Linda was thrilled at the prospect of action but still sobered by the loss of her pony. She prepared a tasty supper in silence. At the end of the meal, she turned to the Indian. "Anyway, Charlie, we brought the two horses for your grandchildren."

"No deal," Charlie declared. "Not a fair trade. You have no horse."

"The trade was made before the palomino was stolen," Bronco stated with finality. "You take the horses to your grandchildren."

After a pause, Charlie gave in. "I will go tomorrow, and be back next morning."

"Maybe we'll have Chica by then," Bob said hopefully. "We're going to keep on searching."

The following day everyone was up for an early breakfast. Soon afterward the group separated. Charlie went in one direction with the quarter horses from Rancho del Sol. Bronco headed for home. Linda and Bob, using two of Charlie's mounts, went more slowly to follow Chica d'Oro's tracks.

It was easy to pick up the hoofprints of the four horses, and to distinguish the filly's from those the three thieves were riding. Her prints were slightly smaller.

The marks, instead of going up a pass in Fossil

Mountain, as Linda and Bob rather expected them to do, swerved right into rough terrain of rocky mounds.

"This is where Bronco and the deputy lost the thieves' trail, I guess," Bob said.

He and Linda rode on, but it became almost impossible to pick up a single track. Finally they stopped to look around.

Linda was bewildered. "Which way shall we go? Straight ahead or up the mountain?"

"It's anybody's guess, but let's try the mountain in the direction of the bottling company."

They started to climb.

After a few minutes, Linda spotted Chica d'Oro's tracks, and those of one other horse, then lost them again. She and her brother assumed the thieves had separated. Linda and Bob hunted fruitlessly and finally came to the foot of a steep, narrow trail.

"Maybe your pony was taken up here and maybe not," Bob said, sighing. "It's too gravelly to see prints."

"Let's try anyway," Linda urged, and they started up the steep path.

Suddenly she gave a little cry and pulled her horse to a stop. Linda slid off, picked a red object from brush beside the path, and held it up triumphantly.

"It's the tassel from Chica d'Oro's hackamore!" she cried jubilantly.

Mountain Tunnel   *12*

Linda clutched the tassel in her hands. "You know," she said happily, "I believe Chica d'Oro scraped this off on the bush so that we could follow her!"

Bob smiled. "Maybe. Anyhow, we know now that we're on the right track."

"We'd better go ahead cautiously," Linda advised. "We may be riding straight into that bunch of horse thieves!"

Bob was worried too. "Perhaps we'd better go back to town and notify the deputy sheriff."

"But my pony could be tied up near here," Linda protested. "Why don't we try to rescue her and make a run for home? If we don't, Chica may be taken farther away."

"I guess you're right," Bob conceded, dismounting. "But before we move on, I want to take a look around here. The thieves or their mounts may have left other clues."

Linda stood lookout while he examined both

sides of the trail, then went off it, into the brush. She could hear him poking among the bushes. For a few minutes, there was silence. Then she heard Bob's long, low whistle.

"He wants me." Linda jumped off her horse and hurried toward the sound. She broke through the brush to a clearing to find her brother kneeling and scooping loose dirt and leaves away from one spot.

"What are you searching for?" Linda asked, rushing over to him.

Bob pointed. "Not searching for something. Locating something. Look!" he cried excitedly. Lying exposed were several colored electric bulbs attached to a cord.

"The mysterious lights! You've found them!" Linda gasped.

Bob nodded. "I almost tripped over them. Whoever is using these as a signal doesn't remove the lights—just keeps them camouflaged by the leaves and dirt."

Brother and sister excitedly decided to follow the bulbs. "This must be part of the line and it starts at the edge of the valley," Bob noted. "That explains how we could see some of the lights from Charlie's cabin."

A sudden thought struck Linda as she and her brother, leading their horses, started off. "You know, if stolen horses *are* being hidden somewhere in this mountain, the thieves might be using these lights after dark to guide them here! Oh, Bob, that could mean this string of bulbs will take us to Chica d'Oro!"

"I hope so," said Bob. "We'd better be on our guard, though, every minute."

He and his sister concentrated on keeping track of the light bulbs. Using sticks, each poked dirt and leaves away from the cord at intervals. Progress became increasingly difficult, since the trail of light bulbs did not follow any well-defined path. The route took the Craigs gradually up the wooded mountainside, around boulders, and through tangled brush.

Finally, Bob offered to hold both horses, while Linda went a little distance ahead to uncover the string of bulbs. This made the going somewhat quicker. But at one spot of especially rocky terrain, she lost the line completely.

"We'll have to backtrack," Bob said, "and start again from the last spot uncovered."

Chafing over the time they had lost, Linda determinedly moved her stick back and forth until she relocated the trail. The eager searchers pushed through the heavy brush, with Linda exposing the electric wire inch by inch.

"Goodness, will we ever come to the end?" she murmured, stopping at last to catch her breath.

"Better take it easy for a minute," Bob advised.

They had just sipped cooling water from their canteens when they heard a crashing through the underbrush.

Linda gasped. "Someone's coming!"

"Down!" Bob ordered. "Behind that bush!"

Linda complied, but whispered fearfully, "They'll see you and the horses!"

Bob remained calmly beside the horses, ready to fend off an attack. The crashing grew louder. The next instant two mountain goats bounded into view. The animals, evidently startled at the sight of Bob, stopped dead for a moment. Linda, with a relieved giggle, stood up quickly. At this, the goats leaped away.

Linda gave a great sigh. "I'll love goats the rest of my life!" she declared.

"I sort of welcomed them myself," Bob said with a grin. He looked up the mountainside. "We're nearly halfway to the top," he observed.

"Let's keep going!" Linda urged, refreshed by the short rest. "We must find out the secret of these lights—and Chica d'Oro!"

"Lead on!" Bob, between the two horses, once more swung into step behind his sister. Her eyes were glued to the ground as she resumed the tedious search for the bulbs.

The minutes seemed like hours, but the weary pair trudged on doggedly. The string of light bulbs snaked around a dense growth of brush and led upward.

"This is certainly a zigzag path," Linda said.

"Probably an old Indian trail," Bob surmised.

Carefully the girl negotiated the steep ascent.

Behind her, Bob had all he could do to keep his own footing and retain his grip on the horses' reins. Presently the searchers approached a heavy growth of bushes directly ahead. Linda skirted them and came to an abrupt halt.

"Bob!" she whispered, astonished. "Look!"

Behind the screen of brush was an opening in the mountainside.

"A tunnel!" he exclaimed. "Maybe an old mine entrance."

"Yes!" returned Linda, shaking with excitement, "and I'll bet the light bulb cord goes into it!" They scratched eagerly at the earth around the entrance and in a few moments Linda held up the cord in silent triumph.

The young sleuths were elated at the discovery. Eagerly they pushed aside several bushes and peered into the yawning black cavern.

"The horse thieves use this tunnel!" Linda guessed. "These lights are a guide to them to bring the stolen animals here at night and hide them inside!"

"Wonder where it leads?" Bob said.

"Let's explore and find out!" Linda proposed, hopeful that the passageway might take her to Chica d'Oro.

"All right," Bob agreed, sensing his sister's thoughts.

Quickly they walked to the wooded growth opposite the tunnel, tied their horses to the trees, and went back to the tunnel. Bob turned on his flashlight and was about to step inside, when Linda grabbed his arm.

"Did you hear that? Horses whinnying!"

"Not in the tunnel?"

"No, somewhere to our left and below us."

Linda and Bob stood still and listened. For a few moments there was silence, but presently the whinnying came again.

"There are horses down the mountain all right," Bob said. "They must have caught a scent of our animals."

"Let's go look at them!" Linda said eagerly. "They might be stolen horses—and Chica d'Oro with them!"

She started off on a run in the direction of the sounds. The whinnying grew louder. At the foot of the mountain, Linda and Bob came face to face with a completely different terrain. Monstrous crags sawtoothed along each side of a crevice.

"The horses are in *there!*" Linda said.

"But this area is patrolled by air. Why weren't the horses seen?" Bob asked.

Linda was already running along the crevice, with Bob in close pursuit. All the while the whinnying noises became steadily more persistent. The excited Craigs raced around a bend. The next instant both skidded to a dead stop at the entrance to a small box canyon. With pounding hearts, they stepped warily inside.

"Bob!" Linda cried. "Over there! Horses! All purebreds."

Brother and sister stood staring at a dozen horses standing side by side beneath a huge overhanging cliff. Their halters were attached to long iron stakes imbedded in the rock wall.

"What a marvelous hiding place!" Linda exclaimed. "No wonder the horses couldn't be seen from the air. That overhang screens them completely."

"Let's have a close look," Bob urged. "Linda, do you realize how much these horses are worth? Thousands of dollars!"

Quickly scanning the area to make certain no one was around, Linda and Bob cautiously approached the group of handsome animals.

"Easy, boy," Linda said softly, going up to one. She was fearful that the sudden presence of Bob and herself might panic the horses. But they remained calm.

Linda's eyes flitted over the animals and beyond them, hoping to spot Chica d'Oro. But the golden pony was not in sight. Every horse was bigger than her palomino.

Oh, dear, what have they done with her? Where is she? Linda wailed inwardly.

Suddenly she noticed in particular a dark bay Morgan. He has the same wonderful conformation as Prince Brownlee, he holds his head erect, and— Excitedly she drew her brother's attention to the

Morgan. "Bob, I have a strong hunch that's Prince —and he's been dyed! And these other horses too. They've all been stolen."

"I agree. But how can we find out for sure?"

Without hesitation, Linda went up to the Morgan. "Hello, Prince Brownlee," she said. "You remember me, don't you?"

The horse's response was immediate. He shook his head and pawed the ground with his right front hoof.

"Exactly what Prince did the first time I saw him!" Linda exclaimed. "Oh, if only we can get him out of here, and take him back to Mr. Brownlee! But first I must find Chica d'Oro!"

"You think she's still hidden somewhere around here?" Bob asked. "She may have been sold."

Linda refused to accept this suggestion. "I think she's nearby, and we must rescue her!"

They speculated on the possible whereabouts of the palomino. Linda had an idea. "Maybe she's at the spot where the thieves dye the horses," she suggested. "I think we ought to go back and investigate the tunnel—perhaps that's the place."

"It's worth a try," Bob conceded.

As they turned to go Linda paused and looked around her, puzzled. "Do you see any running water here?" she asked.

Their eyes scanned the canyon for a spring or a stream.

"No," replied Bob. "How are these horses watered?"

"That's a good question," Linda said. "Let's hurry up to the tunnel and see if we can find some answers."

Bob agreed. "Besides, we'd better get out of this canyon before someone sees us," he warned.

Linda stroked Prince Brownlee's nose. "We'll come back for you and your friends as soon as we can."

She and her brother climbed quickly up the mountainside to the tunnel entrance.

"All set? Let's go!" Bob clicked on his flashlight and led the way inside. Linda, beaming her own light, tiptoed close behind. They found themselves in a medium-sized, rock-walled cavern with an earthen floor. Along one side ran the telltale electric wire, with bulbs attached at intervals.

The Craigs looked about for a light switch, but saw none. Suddenly Linda tensed and pointed to the ground. "Horseshoe prints! They're about Chica's size!"

Bob bent down to study the marks in the hard dirt. "You're right. Those thieves must bring the horses here—and dye them somewhere in the tunnel."

The pulses of both raced. Was the stolen Chica d'Oro within close range?

"Come on!" Linda urged, seeing a passageway ahead.

Deep silence prevailed as the two moved stealth- ily forward. The light from Bob's flash caused eerie shadows to leap and dance over the walls.

Presently the space became narrower. "Ugh! It's weird!" Linda shivered. "Poor Chica—in a place like this!"

In another few seconds, Linda and Bob were brought to a sudden halt. Ahead of them was a door of heavy planks banded by iron strips, with huge iron hinges fastened into the solid rock of the wall. The door handle was a big ringbolt.

"Oh, I hope we can get through!" Linda said in a low voice.

"We'll soon find out," said Bob and stepped up to the huge ring.

He grasped it and strained to open the door, but could not budge it. Linda grabbed the ring with him and pulled. But even their combined strength was not enough to move the door.

"That's odd," Linda remarked. "I just realized there's no lock—the door *should* open, unless it's bolted on the inside."

"It's extremely heavy, and the hinges are rusted," Bob replied. "Maybe that's the trouble."

"I know! Why don't we try horse power?" Linda suggested. "We can tie one end of our lariats to the ringbolt and the other end to the horses, and make *them* pull."

"That's a bright idea!" Bob said approvingly. "But

we'll probably never get them in here. Walking in a dark room is something horses won't do."

"There's always a way of getting a horse to do what you want it to," Linda declared cheerfully. "Once in New York I saw a mounted policeman try to ride his horse into a dark, narrow passageway between buildings. When it wouldn't head in, he backed it in. Let's try!"

"What are we waiting for?" Her brother grinned.

He and his sister hurried outside and took their lariats from the saddles. Bob carried them inside the tunnel. Deftly he knotted an end of each securely to the ring. This done, he gave a low bird call.

Upon hearing the familiar signal, Linda turned her horse around with its rump directly at the entrance. She stood in front of the animal and commanded firmly, "Back! Back! Back!" stepping foward herself as she did so.

The horse obeyed the order perfectly until it was a few paces inside the narrow passageway. Then, suddenly conscious of the black interior, it balked.

"That's far enough," Bob said, and brought the rope ends over. He held Linda's horse until she had backed in the other one.

Swiftly and skillfully the Craigs fastened the lariats securely to the saddle horns and led both the horses forward. Eager to get out into full daylight again, the animals strained full force at the ropes.

Linda watched hopefully while Bob trained his light on the heavy door. The horses continued to tug toward the entrance. At last there came a long, drawn-out grating sound.

"That did it!" Linda exclaimed. "The door's moving!"

In another moment, Bob had untied the ropes from the horses. "We'll take them back outside," he said, "before they get nervous and make a noise."

After fastening their mounts once more to the trees, Linda and Bob retraced their steps to the plank door. It stood open about three inches. Bob now turned off his flashlight as a safety precaution, and when their eyes had become accustomed to the darkness, he slowly pulled back the door.

Linda and Bob peered around it into a pitch-black interior. For a full half-minute they stood motionless, listening for sounds that would indicate a person's presence.

But there was absolute stillness. Linda nudged her brother as a signal to enter. Noiselessly the two slipped into the unknown area beyond the door. The atmosphere felt cold and damp. Not yet wishing to risk a light, Bob and Linda groped their way along, feeling walls and floor with their hands and feet before each step.

"It's all of stone," Linda told herself.

The next moment her hand touched a different substance—glass. Curious, she stooped and ran her fingers over the large object.

I'm sure it's a bottle of some kind, she thought, but what's it doing here? "Bob!" she called softly.

Bob joined her and Linda guided his hand to the bottle-sized object. "Reminds me of a water jug—like those demijohns we saw in the bottling company yard."

He decided to take the chance of turning on his flashlight. The beam stabbed into the blackness and swept over the rugged rocky interior of the tunnel. A demijohn stood on a ledge.

They kept going. Presently there was dim daylight ahead. Trickling from one wall into a pool below was sparkling water. The Craigs looked around and were astonished to see not one, but row after row of heavy, water-filled glass jugs standing near them.

"Bob!" Linda whispered, startled. "We're in the cave behind the bottling company!"

Trapped! 13

Excitedly the Craigs looked around the huge rock chamber at the rows of glass demijohns.

"Here's the water for the horses!" Linda exclaimed softly.

"Of course!" said Bob. "The thieves could fill the jugs here and store them, then carry them down to the box canyon as they're needed."

"Those men Garrant and Worley were lying," Linda went on excitedly. "They're not in the mineral water business. All those jugs and crates and the truck we saw in their yard were a cover-up. Horse stealing is their game!"

"I think you're right," Bob told her. "But we'll have to prove it."

"To think we were talking to them! I wish I'd known then!" Linda said vehemently. "And that awful Luke Poe probably *is* in league with them. Come on," she pleaded. "Let's keep going. We might find Chica d'Oro outside!"

"Not much farther," Bob warned. "We've been lucky up to now. Even the horses' whinnying didn't bring anyone."

Just then his flashlight picked up another tunnel which ran from the cave wall opposite the pool. Linda wanted to investigate it but Bob shook his head.

"We must notify the authorities. We can't wait any longer," he insisted.

"I suppose you're right," Linda said slowly. "But I'd certainly like to know what's in that other tunnel. Please, Bob, just shine your flashlight into it. Then I'll go."

The tunnel was narrower than the other one. It curved sharply a short distance ahead, so nothing was visible beyond the bend. There were small, sharp jutting rocks on the side, and as Bob threw the beam of light on them, Linda gave an exclamation. Quickly she picked a tuft of long white horse hairs from one rock.

"From Chica's mane!" Linda whispered excitedly.

Bob held his light close to the hairs. "That pony sure is bent on being found."

"We're coming, baby!" Linda murmured tensely.

Excited by their discovery, the two went ahead. Presently they came to an enlarged place in the second tunnel, from which ran two branches.

"Now which way?" Linda asked.

"We'd better stick to the main one," Bob answered. "There was most likely a pocket of ore in this spot, and the other two tunnels were dug to bring it all out. They probably don't go deep."

A little farther along Linda whispered, "Listen!"

There were faint echoing noises as if some sort of machine were operating. Then they heard the indistinct sound of voices.

"Let's get out of here!" Bob urged.

They turned back, stepping as lightly as possible. It seemed a long time before they closed the iron door and emerged into the sunlight on the exterior of Fossil Mountain. Their horses stood with locked joints, contentedly dozing.

"Shall we go to the deputy sheriff at Ruddville?" Linda asked, as she and her brother swiftly untied their mounts.

"Too far," Bob replied, swinging into the saddle. "Let's ride to Charlie's."

They started downhill, following the path of the electric wire they had uncovered. "We can make our report to the jeep patrol which is searching for Chica d'Oro, or leave them a message," Bob said.

It was late afternoon when Linda and her brother arrived at the cabin. They had seen nothing of the patrol. Bob took the Indian's binoculars outside and scanned the area.

"The jeep isn't in sight," he told Linda, as he came back into the cabin.

"Maybe they've quit and gone into Ruddville for the night," she suggested.

"Possibly," replied Bob. "But Charlie said the deputy would check here in the morning. We'll leave him a note and a map." Then Bob asked suddenly, "Are you as hungry as I am?"

"Is that a hint?" his sister said with a grimace.

Linda cut slices from the ham that they had brought from home and put them in the oven with canned yams, heated a can of green beans, and opened another containing pears.

When they had finished eating, Linda brought out a large piece of wrapping paper, and with Bob's help started to draw a map on it. They sketched the approach to the narrow mountain trail and showed the line of light bulbs running along the side of it to the tunnel entrance.

Then Linda put in the mineral-water cave of demijohns, and the smaller passageway where they had heard voices. Bob made a drawing of the side of the mountain, showing the water-bottling building with the cave in the slope above it.

"This is pretty terrific," Linda said. "Anyone could follow it."

"Let's leave it tacked on the door so the deputy sheriff will be sure to see it," said Bob.

"Do you mind riding out at dawn?" Linda requested. "I want to try again to find Chica."

Bob nodded. "You bet."

The next morning was a pleasant one, sunny but crisp. Below the cabin, the mountainside was abloom with small, white, starflowers, and the brush was full of tiny, twittering sandpipers.

The Craigs reached Fossil Mountain. As their horses climbed up the steep trail toward the tunnel, Linda took a deep breath. "It's so beautiful and peaceful out here, it's hard to believe wicked people are using the old mountain for mean and dishonest business."

Suddenly Bob raised a quieting hand and pulled his horse off the trail into the brush. Linda followed closely with a questioning glance.

"Someone's up there," Bob murmured. "I saw him move."

They could not distinguish the tunnel entrance, but they knew exactly where it was. As Linda and Bob held their eyes on the location, the figure of a man came into view again.

"They've posted a guard," Linda said in a low voice. She strained to see better. "Maybe he has Chica with him."

Bob pointed to a rock formation among the trees just ahead. "We'll leave our horses behind it and go on foot. Bronco said not to tangle with the men, and I can't let you take any unnecessary chances."

Linda threw her brother a grateful smile. "Okay. We'll see what to do when we get up to the tunnel."

Sister and brother climbed stealthily to the entrance, keeping well to one side of the electric cord trail. When they finally crouched in the brush close to the opening, Linda and Bob saw that the man was Worley.

"I wish we were in that tunnel instead of out here," Linda whispered. "Then we could keep going through to hunt for Chica d'Oro."

"That gives me an idea," Bob said. He picked up a big rock and hurled it toward the path. The rock went crashing down the mountainside through the brush. Worley immediately ran toward the trail to investigate the noise.

"Come on!" Bob whispered, grabbing Linda's hand, and they sprinted quickly into the tunnel. "Don't use your flashlight," he said in an undertone. "Then if Worley comes in here, he won't be able to spot us. We'll have a head start."

Linda followed the suggestion and they managed to get to the iron-hinged door, which now stood open, before turning on their lights. They went ahead quickly.

When they entered the cave back of the bottling company, Linda and Bob stopped and listened. Again, down the tunnel which branched from it, they heard the faint noise of a machine.

"I believe it's a generator," said Bob, "but I'd like to get a glimpse of it."

"And I want to see if my palomino is there," Linda added.

They inched along past the two smaller branches, and then noticed radiance from beyond the curve.

Peering cautiously around it, they saw that the tunnel ended in a large rock chamber. In one corner of the brilliantly lit spot stood a squat power generator. It was making the noise Bob and Linda had heard. Strung across the ceiling and on the walls were rows of high wattage electric light bulbs.

Near one side, Garrant was seated at a table, writing. Luke Poe slouched against the wall behind him and watched. He was as unshaven and poorly dressed as the day he had tried to steal Chica d'Oro.

Garrant said with a self-satisfied smile, "We've got just about enough buyers' names now to make a nice haul."

"How many more horses do we have to sell?" asked Poe. "I'd like to get out of this squirrel hole."

"You just sit tight in your skin," snarled Garrant. He tapped his head. "I'm the brains. I say what we do."

"Sure, you're the big brain," Poe replied, "but I got you the water-bottling works to hide behind, didn't I?"

Garrant gave him a condescending look of appreciation. "Of course, it takes a team to work a deal like this."

With a rough guffaw, Poe slapped his knee. "I'm laughing at old Worley out there, scraping dirt off and on those colored lights."

Garrant grinned with amusement. "My master stroke. Since there's nothing showing above ground unless we want it to, nobody's going to catch on to our little scheme. Who'd guess it's to guide the horses to this spot at night after we've stolen 'em?"

"And whose idea was it to dye the horses?" Poe asked. "Mine!"

He pointed with pride to the opposite side of the chamber. There lay a spray gun, next to several large black-stained paint containers.

Linda and Bob nudged one another. *This* was the place for dyeing the horses!

Garrant scowled. "Yeah, but you could have brought the law down on us when you went after the yellow horse."

"That animal was worth money," the slouching man retorted. "If I could pick it up for nothing, who's to say I'm not the smartest one?"

"You're not," Garrant snapped, "because you fumbled it. When I took you and Worley to steal the horse we not only succeeded, but made the theft serve a purpose."

"Sure, you had Gus and Ed take the pickup down to the ranch with the dog and the ransom note the same night. That really got the law after us," Poe replied sullenly.

"The law is out in the valley picking daisies," said the leader smugly, checking off the last item on a record sheet.

"And why did you and Worley steal that chestnut Morgan in daylight when he had a rider on him?" Poe needled. "Was that the smart, quiet way to do the job?"

"We have the horse. That's all that matters," Garrant answered shortly.

"We also have the girl and her brother on our trail," Poe retorted.

"We're rid of the Craigs," Garrant said icily. "They're so busy looking for the palomino they have no time to look for us."

Under the ringleader's cold eyes, Poe shifted. "Worley better not catnap guarding that entrance," he muttered.

Linda and Bob glanced at each other with a quick grin.

"How's the water supply?" Garrant asked. "Many full jugs out there?"

"Couldn't say right off," the henchman replied. "A lot, I guess."

"Guessing isn't good enough," Garrant said harshly. He picked up a flashlight from the table and tossed it to the other man. "We'll go count. And don't turn on any lights."

With Garrant close behind, Poe started to shamble across the room toward the Craigs.

"We must get away from here," whispered Bob.

"Into a branch tunnel!" Linda replied quickly.

They skimmed to the junction on tiptoe, and hurried into the black opening on the left. Not daring to use flashlights, they felt their way along until they saw a dim light which came from beyond a curve.

Stepping gingerly, they investigated. Suddenly Linda almost cried aloud.

Before them, in a small lantern-lighted dugout, they saw Chica d'Oro tethered to an iron stake driven into the dirt floor!

The palomino recognized Linda and Bob at the same time and gave a joyous whinny. Linda rushed up to her and held one hand over the horse's nose, saying, "Quiet, baby! Quiet!" Chica d'Oro kept up a soft nickering as she nuzzled her owner's head and neck.

Suddenly Linda and Bob heard running footsteps in the tunnel. As the Craigs whirled, Poe and Garrant burst in upon them.

"I told you a horse doesn't talk to itself," Garrant exclaimed to his henchman. A look of amazement changed to a cold, calculating smile directed at the girl and boy. "So your palomino led you into a trap!" he gloated. "Fine! Fine! This time you don't get away from us!"

The Rope Trick 14

For a moment, Bob and Linda faced their two captors in shocked silence. Chica d'Oro, however, snorted and pawed at the hard dirt floor with a forefoot. From the instant Luke Poe and Garrant had entered the dugout, she had quivered nervously, tossed her head, and switched her tail.

Linda remembered well the day Poe had attempted to steal the palomino, when the horse had reared and struck at him with her hooves. Now the filly was well tethered down so that she could not repeat the onslaught, but as Garrant took a step toward her, she whinnied shrilly.

Linda's dark eyes snapped. "The pony doesn't like you," she told the ringleader, and Bob added, "You must have tried to hurt her."

"She remembers me all right," the man replied grimly. "She'll follow my commands or I'll beat her."

Linda drew in her breath, and wrapped her arm tightly around the palomino's neck.

"She'd kill you if you ever struck her," the girl said hotly.

Disdain twisted the man's face, but in his eyes was a flicker of fear like Linda had seen the day Chica d'Oro had fought Poe off.

Both men are afraid of her, Linda thought; they know that if she ever gets free she'll strike at them.

With a chill, she remembered that the men had carried guns when they stole the palomino from Bronco. If they could not control the animal, they might shoot her! Linda's concern for the pony was so great she had no thought of her own predicament.

"Hand over those flashlights!" Garrant ordered.

As Linda and Bob obeyed, the sound of hurrying, stumbling footsteps along the main tunnel drew their attention. The two men listened sharply for a moment.

"Worley," Garrant said.

"We're in here," Poe called out.

Worley burst in upon them with a worried look. Then he stopped short and stared bug-eyed at the sister and brother. "How'd they get in here?"

"That's what you'd better tell us if you want to save your skin," said Garrant icily.

"I found a couple of horses out there," explained Worley. "Didn't know whose they were. They're different from the ones these two rode here from the ranch. Thought some mounted deputies might have come this close. I rushed in to warn you."

Garrant turned to Bob and demanded, "How did you get in here?"

The boy replied evenly, "The same way those daisy-picking deputies are going to!"

"You know too much," growled Poe.

"We know that Garrant is the leader of you horse thieves," said Linda.

"How'd you find that out?" asked Poe, surprised.

"You just told me," she said triumphantly. Garrant scowled at Poe angrily for being so gullible.

"How can you prove it?" Worley asked Linda.

"Lots of ways," she answered. "Strings of colored electric lights, cans of dye, a spray gun, and a box canyon—"

The men's mouths dropped open in astonishment. Finally Poe collected his wits and asked, "What are we going to do about these two snoopers?"

"They're evidently on to our whole scheme," Worley declared.

Garrant swaggered a bit and said harshly, "It doesn't matter what they know because they are never going to get out of here alive!"

Linda's heart sank. Bob, however, stood steadfast, his crackling brown eyes straight on the ringleader.

"You're too late," he said. "Before we came out

this morning, we left a note for the sheriff's deputies, who are due any minute. We also left a map showing exactly how to get here, the location of the cave with the full water jugs, and the generator and dyeing equipment in the rock chamber."

"I'm getting out of here," blurted Poe.

"Don't move!" barked Garrant, drawing a revolver from a shoulder holster. "These two kids are lying. That was just a try to save their skins."

"We're not lying," Linda retorted. "We've been here before."

"You hear that?" Worley exclaimed.

"It doesn't matter," snapped the ringleader. "We'll get those horses out of the box canyon and take them down through the woods. Nobody will see us. Let the sheriff's men have this place."

"Have you gone loco?" Poe spoke up. "We'd better let those horses in the canyon loose and scram as fast as we can! We don't want to be nabbed with stolen goods."

"I'm not going to get caught," Garrant declared. "The deputies won't make it here this early. First I want to clean out all our records, starting with my desk. Poe, you go down to the canyon and bring three horses up to the mine entrance. I'll meet you there and load the papers into the saddlebags. We'll ride those three mounts and lead the others. Worley, you stay here and guard these two prisoners of ours." He turned sharply and went into the tunnel, followed by Poe.

His forehead beaded with sweat, Worley pulled an empty box up to the entrance and sat down. "How come you two didn't fall into that quicksand?" he asked in a surly tone.

"We did," said Linda, hugging Chica d'Oro, whose nervousness had ebbed as soon as Poe and Garrant had left. "But we got out."

"You're too smart for your own good," growled Worley.

"Why did you do all that damage at Rancho del Sol?" Bob asked. "What did you expect to accomplish?"

"It was to get you two and your grandfather back to the place and keep you there taking care of it," replied Worley.

"Why didn't you pick up the five hundred dollars we left in the mailbox at the hamburger stand?" Linda questioned him.

"Aw, I wanted to," Worley admitted, "but Garrant found out there were sheriff's deputies staked out all over the place. We weren't going to be taken in for chicken feed when we can make hundreds of thousands of dollars." He looked at Linda and Bob curiously. "How come you didn't give up looking for that yaller horse when it wasn't left at the Silver Sage Ranch?"

"Because I love her," Linda replied. "I would never give up looking for her."

"She's just a horse," mumbled Worley. "You could have got yourself another one."

"There isn't another Chica d'Oro and you know it," Linda said angrily. "Otherwise you wouldn't have stolen her."

"She's been more trouble 'n she's worth," Worley grumbled. "Poe saw her first, one day when he was passing the Injun's cabin, and he made up his mind to have her. After that, he spied on the place for days, looking for a safe chance to take the horse. He was up at Charlie's that Sunday when you arrived. That's when he heard you say you'd come to investigate the lights and look for the Morgan horse."

"So you decided to get rid of us."

Worley nodded. "Garrant decided the best way was to see that you had an accident. So Poe and me dug the burro trap. If that didn't work, we figured to try something else."

"Was that you," Bob asked, "who tried to run us off the road in a car?"

"Sure. I waited on a side road and Poe signaled me from the hilltop when you were coming." Worley laughed. "Guess that shook you up, didn't it?"

"You were pretty careless to leave your trademark in the dust there and in Chica's corral," Bob said.

"What do you mean?" the man asked resentfully.

"The star mark on your boot sole," Bob replied, "or was it your companion's?"

Quickly the man looked at the bottom of his boot. "I didn't know it was there," he said gloomily.

"What's in that other branch tunnel?" asked Linda.

Worley looked at her sharply and set his lips. "I'm through talking," he declared.

"He doesn't know, Linda," Bob said quickly. "Garrant apparently doesn't let the little fish in on everything."

"Not so fast," Worley protested. "Garrant isn't holding anything back on me. We're all in this together. Poe and I are just as smart as he is." Worley chewed his under lip, then blurted, "Sure, I know what's in the tunnel. No harm in telling you, because you're not getting out of here. There's a dugout like this one with bags of oats in it. Don't dare leave 'em where they can be seen."

"I'm tired of standing up," Linda said a few minutes later. She pulled one of the empty boxes up against the side of the dugout behind Chica d'Oro.

"Don't you try to pull anything, or you'll be sorry," Worley warned her.

"I just want to sit down," Linda answered with a sigh.

"That's a good idea," the man said. "You sit down and stay down. You too, young fellow."

Both Bob and Linda sat on the box. The girl leaned her head back wearily. Then her eyes widened. In the silence, she could faintly hear the sound of the electric generator.

She turned her head, and saw in the dimness that planks, not dirt and rock wall, were behind her.

Through a hair-wide crack between the boards, she now noticed brighter light.

Bob was sitting forward with his hands clasped in front of him, pondering their situation. Linda touched his arm and motioned for him to put his ear against the plank partition.

He said in an undertone, "This dugout is next to the rock chamber." Then he leaned forward again and called, "Say, Worley, why did they board up the end of the dugout?"

"The tunnel made a bad draft. We were afraid of fire." Then the man asked suspiciously, "Why do you care?"

"Just curious," Bob replied casually.

Linda murmured to her brother, "We must get out of here! But how?"

"I know," Bob replied softly. "We'll stand up and stretch. Leave the rest to me." He stood up.

"What are you trying to do?" barked Worley.

"Just stretching," Bob replied, and yawned. "I'm getting stiff."

"Me, too," said Linda, rising.

"Hey, look at that dirt!" Bob cried suddenly. "It's coming down fast! Look at it, Worley, over on the side. There's going to be a cave-in. We'll be buried!"

Worley, who had regarded the boy suspiciously at first, now stood up, asking quickly, "Where do you see it?"

"Over there," Bob exclaimed, pointing.

The man took his glance off the prisoners just long enough for Bob to snatch the box he and Linda had been using and hurl it at Worley. The box struck the man broadside, and he lurched back a step against the crate on which he had been seated. He lost his balance and went down with a crash which knocked him unconscious. Worley's gun had dropped from his hand. Linda kicked it hard and the weapon skidded behind a coil of rope.

Quickly Bob grabbed up a length of the rope. He tied Worley's hands behind him and bound his ankles securely together. Then he took out the man's kerchief and tied it tightly over his mouth so he could not call out when he regained consciousness.

Linda turned to Chica d'Oro. "We'll be back for you soon, baby."

"Come on!" Bob urged, grabbing his sister's hand.

They ran out of the branch tunnel into the main one, across the mineral springs cave, and into the longer tunnel that led to freedom. A moment later the Craigs could hear men pounding in pursuit.

As Linda and Bob sprinted faster down the dark passageway, Garrant suddenly loomed up in front of them. He made a grab for the sister and brother, catching each by an arm. His fingers were like steel vises. The men called Gus and Ed panted up and also seized them.

Garrant eyed his captives and laughed shortly. "Surprised you, eh? I just packed one load of papers on my horse. Lucky I had to return for another batch, wasn't it? Gus, Ed!" he barked. "Take these kids back!"

Followed by the ringleader, the two men hustled Linda and Bob to the small dugout. Worley was now straining at his bonds and making sounds in his throat. Garrant threw him a contemptuous look as he tossed a rope to Gus and one to Ed.

"Tie up these kids!" he ordered. "Make it fast!"

As the men obeyed, Chica d'Oro began to move around fretfully. Garrant cast her an uneasy look.

Just then Poe came in. "Hey, Worley," he said, "the horses are all . . ." He stopped short and stared at the trussed-up man.

"Get him free!" commanded Garrant.

Poe jumped to oblige.

"Hurry!" Garrant snapped nervously. "We've got to move!"

Linda and Bob, bound hand and foot, were pushed down on the empty box where they had been before.

"You're not leaving the palomino, are you?" Poe asked Garrant.

"I am," the leader snapped. "There's no time to bother with it. Follow me. I have two more jobs before we go." The three men hurried off.

"Sorry, Linda," Bob whispered. "I thought Garrant was still in the office and we could manage Poe alone if we met him."

"Never mind," his sister replied. "Let's try to

hear what the men are saying. They're doing something in the next room!"

She and her brother pressed their ears against the board partition and heard Garrant's voice. "There are two jeeps full of sheriff's men heading across the valley in this direction. They'll be arriving before long. We'll set a stick of dynamite to cause an earth slide in here, and then run."

"Let's go out the cave entrance," Poe said anxiously. "It's closer."

"Of course," Garrant replied. "We'll go around the mountain and pick up our horses at the mine tunnel. Poe," he ordered sharply, "set this charge with a good long fuse so we can get away before the explosion goes off."

Linda and Bob were horrified. "If I could just get at my knife!" gasped Bob, struggling against his bonds.

The weapon was clasped to his belt in a leather case. Linda tried to work it loose with her tied hands. She could reach the case but could not move her fingers enough to pull open the latched-down flap of stiff leather.

"Oh, I can't do it!" she wailed softly. Then Linda exclaimed in a whisper, "I know something else to try."

She hopped to Chica d'Oro's head, saying, "Untie the rope, golden girl. Untie my hands." She pushed them up against the pony's nose.

The filly nuzzled them. Then, feeling the rope,

she started working at it with her nimble lips and strong biting teeth, as Linda had seen her do playfully.

"Hurry, baby, hurry!" Linda begged.

Suddenly they heard Poe say sharply, "All set, boss."

"Cut off the generator!" Garrant commanded. The humming noise ceased and the thread of light between the planks went out.

"Let's go!" said Garrant.

Linda and Bob heard the men running from the rock chamber and knew that the fuse had been lighted.

"It will burn fast!" Linda cried in panic. "Oh, Chica d'Oro, hurry, hurry!"

An Arabian Princess   15

Linda trembled as Chica d'Oro's teeth picked at the rope around her wrists.

"Is she getting it?" Bob asked unsteadily.

"I—I think so," his sister answered.

Then it seemed to Linda as if the rope had loosened a little. Next Chica got a firm hold of a strand with her teeth and shook her head. The girl thought her wrist was cut in two, but in the next instant the rope fell away and her hands were free.

"Thanks, baby," she gasped and hop-jumped over to Bob, quickly drew out his knife, and cut his hands and feet free. He grabbed the lantern and bolted from the dugout.

Linda freed her own ankles and severed her pony's tether. "I'll be right back for you," she promised the filly and groped her way after Bob.

She hurried down the branch tunnel and up the other passage into the big chamber. She could hear the fuse sputtering and on the rock wall across from her was a flickering glow. In the eerie light, Bob knelt beside the generator.

"It's here!" he called. "Bring the knife!" Linda handed him the blade and he swiftly sliced off the burning tip.

The girl heaved a long shuddering sigh. Bob leaned back against the wall, rubbed his hand over his forehead, and croaked, "Whew!"

After a moment, he fumbled for the generator and the room was flooded with light. Less than two feet away lay sticks of dynamite. Just then Bob and Linda heard hoofbeats in the tunnel. Chica d'Oro had followed Linda in spite of the darkness.

"In here, Chica," she called, "in here!"

At that instant, Garrant dashed in from the tunnel. He pushed Bob and Linda aside, grabbed for the fuse, and gave an exclamation of relief at seeing it out.

Then he turned on them with a wrathful face. "You've got the lawmen swarming around this mountain," he said bitterly. "They nabbed the others, but not me. I'm getting away! First, though, I'm going to even the score with you."

As he took a threatening step toward the Craigs, there was a shrill whinny behind them. The palomino had entered the rock chamber! In her intelligent brown eyes flashed the hatred she held for him. Now she reared and struck the man a stunning blow. He fell to the ground.

Swiftly Linda and Bob knelt beside the motionless Garrant. "He's unconscious," Bob said.

Linda hugged Chica d'Oro and murmured praises to her. Suddenly she and Bob heard men's voices and hurried footsteps in the main tunnel. A few moments later Charlie Tonka and a couple of deputies came into the rock chamber.

Charlie spotted Garrant on the floor and darted to the Craigs. "You all right?" he asked.

"Yes," Bob replied, "but it was close." He held up the fuse and pointed to the dynamite.

"Chica saved our lives," Linda declared and told what the horse had done. The deputies looked at the filly with wonder.

"Good young'un," Charlie said, patting her.

Just then Deputy Wilkins strode in from the tunnel. "Who's that?" he asked, seeing the unconscious man.

"His name's Garrant," Bob said. "He's the mastermind of this ring of horse thieves."

Wilkins spotted a jug of the mineral water standing in a corner. He picked it up and hurled the full contents into Garrant's face. The man rolled his head back and forth, groaning.

"On your feet," Wilkins commanded.

Under the deputy's firm urging, the captive groggily stood up. His smoldering eyes fell on Linda and Chica d'Oro. "You!" he snarled.

Wilkins snapped bracelets on his wrists and gave the prisoner a push. To the others he added, "You all come along, too. We want to get some matters cleared up for the record."

He marshaled Garrant into the tunnel, and a few minutes later the Craigs and Charlie followed with Chica d'Oro at their heels.

"Good thing you left the note and map," the Indian said. "Two deputies checked at my place the same time I got there. They used a two-way radio to call Deputy Wilkins in Ruddville. He brought his men here through the cave mouth. He told us to go around to the other side of the mountain and come in through the mine entrance. We sped in the jeep to the bottom of the hill, climbed the trail, and hurried fast into the tunnel."

"Garrant saw the deputies coming down the valley. That's what started the fireworks," Bob said.

Charlie cocked his head with a sly smile. "Señor Bronco will be very proud when he hears what you did."

Linda smiled at Charlie. "Now you can go back to riding your pipeline without strange lights and horse thieves to worry you."

The Indian's face turned glum. "It will be dull."

"But now that you've given the horses to your grandsons," Linda continued enthusiastically, "you can have the boys with you sometimes."

A quick, happy smile wreathed the Indian's face. "That will be okay. They are fine boys. I will show them how to be good riders."

When the group came out of the cave mouth, they saw below three jeeps and several sheriff's deputies outside the water-bottling building.

Linda let Chica d'Oro's tie rope loose so that the horse could get down the steep slope in her own way. She chose to slide on her rump. Linda followed on the narrow foot path, slipping on her boot soles most of the way, as did the others.

They went in the wide back door of the building. Poe and Worley sat glumly on the daybed, manacled together. Next to them were Gus and Ed. Garrant sat opposite in a straight chair. The prisoners were advised of their legal rights but they agreed they did not want counsel.

Deputy Wilkins, standing before the men, said, "You might as well talk. We know that you, Garrant, are a wanted horse thief in many states. We have your picture on file."

The three men sat in stubborn silence as Wilkins went on, "Now then, the dam was government property. Which of you blew that up?"

"I didn't have anything to do with it," Poe blurted out.

"I didn't blow it," growled Garrant, as Gus and Ed shook their heads.

"You?" the officer asked Worley.

The tall henchman was quaking. "He gave the orders." He thrust out a finger toward Garrant.

"I gave no orders to blow up the dam," snarled the ringleader.

"You said to get rid of the snoopers," Worley babbled.

"Talk!" the officer ordered. "It will go easier for you."

A young deputy seated at the table was taking rapid notes in shorthand.

Worley shifted uneasily. "After we found out these kids were on our trail, Poe and me took turns spying on the Injun's cabin. One night I sneaked up to an open window and heard the Craigs talk about camping on the mountain. Next day I hid behind a big granite rock and saw them riding past."

"And followed us!" Bob exclaimed.

Worley nodded. "With my binoculars I saw them bedded down on a slope a mile below the dam. So I blew it. They ought to have been drowned." He turned, sour-faced, to Linda and Bob. "How come you got away?"

"Chica d'Oro awakened us," Linda replied. "She saved our lives."

"That horse again!" Garrant grumbled.

Linda had let the filly loose to nibble about in back of the building. At the moment, Chica d'Oro stood at the door, looking in curiously. Linda blew her a kiss. The pony nickered and turned back to her foraging. As she did, a tall deputy came in the front door, carrying a pile of papers.

"What did you find?" asked Wilkins.

"Garrant and his gang have been living in the Mineral Springs Lodge," the man replied. "They had a file there of all their operations, with the names of the owners and the stolen horses listed."

Garrant groaned. "I was going to clean out that file, but didn't have time."

"Was Prince Brownlee one of the horses?" Linda asked quickly.

"Yes," the tall deputy replied.

"I knew it! I've seen him. He's been dyed!"

"We've seen a number of purebreds," Bob added. "They're hidden not far from here."

"What!" Wilkins exclaimed.

Linda told about the box canyon with its overhanging rocks, under which the horses were prisoners.

Wilkins turned to Garrant. "You're going with us to identify those horses."

The thief tried to protest but was prodded along. Linda led the way back through the tunnel with Bob, Charlie, Wilkins, and Garrant following. The excited girl ran most of the way down the hill, through the winding crevice, and into the box canyon.

At once, the captive horses began to caper, rear, and snort. Linda thought, I'll bet they recognize this horrid horse thief!

She, Bob, and Charlie tried to soothe the panicking animals. It was not until Linda walked up to the Morgan, once golden chestnut, now dark bay, and said, "Prince Brownlee, boy, I'm going to take you home," that he quieted down. His example seemed to calm the other animals.

"The capture of these thieves was a fine piece of work on your part, young lady, and yours, too, Bob," said Wilkins. "And now, Garrant, who are the owners of the other horses?"

The thief tried to bargain. "Will you guarantee me a light sentence if I tell you?"

"If you don't tell, we'll find out anyway," was the curt reply.

Garrant hesitated a moment. "All right," he said grudgingly. He pointed to the nearest horse. "From Hilltop X ranch in Nevada. The next is from the Bide-a-wee Stables—"

As he droned on, Linda went over to Prince Brownlee and untied him. She caressed his neck and laid her cheek against it. Finally she said, "Bob, help me up, will you? I'm going to ride him to meet Chica d'Oro."

Bob offered his hand as a stirrup and Linda swung onto Prince Brownlee's back. The horse did not move until the rider nudged him with her knees. She guided him up the hill, across the top of the tunnel, and down to the front of the bottling company plant.

The others had cut through the tunnel and were waiting for her. She noted that all the prisoners were manacled and ready to be driven off to jail. Linda was told that the sheriff's men would take care of the other stolen horses until their owners could come for them.

"Charlie," Bob added, "will pick up his horses near the mine entrance where we left them. He'll ride one and lead the other back to the cabin. You and I can take Chica and Prince Brownlee. Are you ready to go?"

Linda dismounted. "After all this excitement, I'm starving. Is there any food here?"

"Plenty," said Wilkins. "Help yourselves. The gang won't be needing it!"

"Thank you," said Linda, and found cans of biscuits, meat, and juices in the kitchen of the former hotel.

After she and Bob had eaten a snack, they rode back to the cabin. Early the next morning the Craigs packed their gear on the horses and said good-bye to their Indian friend.

"We'll come back to see you, Charlie," the girl called.

With Linda mounted on Chica d'Oro and Bob on Prince Brownlee, they made the long ride back to Rancho del Sol. Bronco strode out to greet them with Doña Mallory right behind him. He hugged Linda and exclaimed, "By jump, you found your horse and Mr. Brownlee's too, and solved the mystery of the strange lights!" Then he shook hands proudly with Bob while their grandmother beamed on the two and kissed them.

"Deputy Randall called," said Bronco, "and gave

us the news. Wilkins had phoned him. Now Mr. Brownlee is waiting to hear from us. I'll give him a ring at once."

The best stall, which opened out on a large fenced paddock of permanent pasture, awaited Chica d'Oro. It had been heaped with clean bedding straw, and Linda made the filly comfortable there before she hurried into the house.

A short time later the very grateful Mr. Brownlee arrived. He was dismayed to see that his prizewinning horse had been dyed, but remarked that the artificial color would gradually disappear.

Everyone gathered in the living room to hear Linda and Bob tell their story, including Cactus Mac and Luisa, who stood in the doorway with a mixing spoon in her hand.

When the account was finished and all questions answered, Linda added, "But now I have a greater mystery to solve. I just must find out Chica d'Oro's lineage so that I can have her registered."

Bronco rubbed his chin. "That might prove tough, but go to it."

The next day, as soon as the family was up, representatives from the press, a newsmagazine, and photographers arrived. Once again Linda and Bob recounted their adventures and the part the golden horse had played.

There were no more visitors until the middle of the afternoon. Linda was with her pony in the paddock when she saw a station wagon drive up beside the corral. In it was Mrs. Larsen from the Silver Sage Ranch. The tall, handsome woman strode over to Linda, smiling.

"I heard on the radio about your adventure," she said, "and thought I'd come to invite you to enter Chica d'Oro in the Parade Class for the Perpetual Trophy in our next horse show."

"Oh, I'd love to," Linda answered excitedly. "Tell me more about it."

"The trophy has to be won three times in succession in order to keep it," Mrs. Larsen explained. She smiled. "It's a handsome, engraved silver tray."

"Of course I'll enter Chica d'Oro," Linda replied. "I'd love to!"

"Fine." Mrs. Larsen took a small notebook and pencil from her purse. "Now if you'll just give me the names of her dam and sire for publicity, I'll sign you up."

A shadow fell over Linda's face. "I don't have the names yet. But I'm going to get them."

"Oh, dear," Mrs. Larsen said. "I presumed that the horse's registration had been taken care of. I'm sorry, Linda, but the class is open only to registered parade horses." Then she said pleasantly, "Later some time, when you have had it done, let us see you at the Silver Sage show."

"Oh, you will," the girl assured her.

After the woman left, Linda stroked Chica

d'Oro's neck with a tender hand and told her, "I'll get you registered, baby, don't you worry!"

Linda obtained a copy of the registration book from the state Arabian association, and started the long check-out. She began writing to each owner of Arabian horses, asking if he had lost a mare at the time Charlie had found Chica's mother. Answers came in, but they were always no.

Linda thought of almost nothing else until diverted one day by a visit from Mr. Brownlee. She had not seen him ride in, but was called to the living room to meet him.

"I've brought a present for that golden horse, who I think deserves high honors," he told her and led the way to the back patio.

There Cactus Mac held Chica d'Oro, who was standing like a golden statue, adorned with a gleaming silver saddle, martingale, and bridle. At sight of Linda, the filly whinnied joyously, tossed her mane proudly, and tapped the brick floor with a dainty forefoot.

Linda was almost breathless with excitement, but managed to exclaim, "How absolutely beautiful! Oh, Mr. Brownlee, how can I ever thank you enough?"

The caller was smiling but held up his hand. "I have something for Bob, too. Guess you can use this at college."

The gift proved to be an electronic traveling clock

that would keep perfect time under all conditions. Bob was as overwhelmed as his sister.

While all this was going on a car pulled into Rancho del Sol. A big square-jawed man stepped out and introduced himself as Tom Wister from Nevada. He came to the point at once.

"I've read the accounts of your remarkable palomino with great interest. I believe she is the colt of an Arabian mare in foal that was stolen from me a little less than three years ago."

Linda listened breathlessly.

"It's possible," Mr. Wister continued, "that my horse was brought to California, then escaped her captor. She could open almost any latch. Ranashi was her name. She came of a fine Arabian blood line, and the sire of her foal was Golden Supreme, my famed saddlebred stallion. Now, if I can see the filly, I think I can verify my claim. Every colt of Golden Supreme's has a jag in the blaze between the eyes."

"She has! Oh, she has!" Linda said aloud, but thought in panic, He'll claim Chica d'Oro!

With a sinking heart, she led Mr. Wister and the others to the paddock. Linda watched the big man's eyes narrow when he saw the pony, and he nodded. There was silence as he stroked the filly's nose gently and nodded again.

"She's the one, I'm sure," he said. "Looks just like her dam except for the jag. But I wish we had positive proof."

Linda took a deep breath. "You'll sell her to me, won't you?" she asked.

"No," the man said quietly. "No." He looked from the horse to Linda. "She's yours. You've earned her."

Suddenly Bob excused himself and raced off. He was gone only a few minutes. When he returned, his face wore an expansive smile. "I have proof!" he exclaimed. "Chica d'Oro's dam *was* Ranashi. I asked the sheriff to look in Garrant's records of stolen horses. The name was there. Garrant and his gang operated for a while in Nevada. They brought Ranashi down here, but she escaped from them. When they found the mare, she was badly hurt, so they abandoned her."

"And that's when Indian Charlie found Ranashi!" Linda exclaimed.

The whole group was exultant and made a great fuss over Chica d'Oro. Mr. Wister pulled a registration blank and the address of the palomino registry from his pocket and handed them to Linda. "I like to keep track of my stock," he told her. "If you would just send me a picture of this horse sometime, I'd appreciate it."

"I will," Linda promised with tears of happiness in her eyes. "Thank you. Thank you."

As Bronco and Grandmother Mallory escorted the visitors back to the house, Linda waved the registration blank before Chica d'Oro's eyes.

"We've won!" she sang out. "We've won!"

THE LINDA CRAIG® SERIES
By Ann Sheldon

The Palomino Mystery #1
The Clue on the Desert Trail #2
The Secret of Rancho del Sol #3
The Mystery of Horseshoe Canyon #4
The Mystery in Mexico #5
The Ghost Town Treasure #6
The Haunted Valley #7
Secret of the Old Sleigh #8
The Emperor's Pony #9

You Will Also Enjoy

NANCY DREW MYSTERY STORIES®
By Carolyn Keene

The Triple Hoax #57
The Flying Saucer Mystery #58
The Secret in the Old Lace #59
The Greek Symbol Mystery #60
The Swami's Ring #61
The Kachina Doll Mystery #62
The Twin Dilemma #63
Captive Witness #64
Mystery of the Winged Lion #65
Race Against Time #66
The Sinister Omen #67
The Elusive Heiress #68
Clue in the Ancient Disguise #69
The Broken Anchor #70
The Silver Cobweb #71
The Haunted Carousel #72